12-2011

Ruth Ellen,

Enjoy my Book

Shiloh
Speaks

Love & Licks,

SHILOH
SPEAKS

D1457035

SHILOH SPEAKS
© 2011 by Jerry Hill and Colleen Rae
All rights reserved.

Cover Art Design & Photo by Jerry Hill
Book Design – CreateSpace Publishing

ISBN: 1466213809
ISBN-13: 9781466213807

Some names and places have been changed for expediency.
Names of restaurants and towns do exist or did exist at one time.

Shiloh Speaks

A Therapy Dog's Memoir of Unconditional Love

By Shiloh
With Jerry Hill And Colleen Rae

MOSTLY TRUE TAILS

"People only see what they are prepared to see."

—Ralph Waldo Emerson

"Your imagination is your preview of life's coming attractions."

—Albert Einstein

"Do not neglect to show hospitality to strangers, for by this some have entertained Angels without knowing it."

—Hebrews 13:2

Contents

Why Write This Book?

While riding on the golf course, a good friend, Larry, shared that he was about to turn sixty-five. Since I was ten years his senior, he asked, "What happens now?"

I announced he would have to plan his life's legacy.

He countered quickly, referring to the golden retriever riding between us in the cart.

"How about Shiloh? He'll probably go before us."

Shiloh had volunteered for eleven years as a Therapy Dog and it was a great question I hadn't considered for this amazing Dog.

"Any ideas, Larry?"

"Sure, write his memoir. He's had a remarkable career, and it would make a great book."

"Larry, I've never written anything in my life and the same applies to Shiloh."

"Have my wife, Colleen, help you," Larry said. "She's an author."

And the rest is in this book…

Shiloh, Colleen, and I hope you'll enjoy our labor of love.

—Jerry Hill

This book is dedicated to all the Dogs of the world.

Shiloh

· This book was written as a memoir
by Shiloh, a golden retriever
through the words of his master, Jerry Hill.
There is no intent to deceive or to be dishonest.
If one can read about vampires in romance novels,
one can accept that Dogs talk.

CHAPTER 1

Therapy Dog

The work of a Therapy Dog is an intimate journey
between the Dog and the person he visits.

—Shiloh

I laid my head down on the small boy's lap. This brought a smile to Joshua's lips. His frail hand crept across the blanket and gently stroked my head.

Joshua listened to my master Jerry tell the hospice nurse that I had been involved in therapy work for over ten years.

"Do you need therapy, Shiloh?" the boy asked. "Are you sick too?"

I wanted to tell Joshua that I give therapy to those who are elderly, sick and ready to make their final transition from this life to the great beyond, but since I can't communicate with words, I had to let Jerry explain. I'm the only Dog in America who has recorded over one thousand hospice visits. I will tell Joshua's story later in this book.

My master trained me to be a Therapy Dog. I have the sensitivity and compassion to spend enough time with a person in a hospital, hospice facility, or nursing home to give comfort before their final journey.

Jerry Hill thinks I'm a beautiful golden retriever, and many people agree with him. I'm not being vain; it's a fact. I am twelve years old, and before I make my final transition, I want to share with you something about my life and how I have volunteered my time in service to others.

My master and I have a special bond. We have spent so much time together and have been friends for so long that we can read each other's thoughts. Because of this, Jerry is my spokesperson in the world in which we live, and in this book I am speaking through him.

By now you are probably thinking, "How can a Dog write a book?" Stretch your imagination. Think outside the kennel. I want you to see things through my eyes. What you're about to read is 98 percent factual. You'll have to guess about the other 2 percent.

In the beginning, Jerry found me through an ad in the *Traverse City Record Eagle*. I've heard him tell this story a hundred times, so I can share it easily. Perhaps I've added a few embellishments, but that's the prerogative of an author.

In 1998, Jerry was hunting near Traverse City, Michigan, on the 3,350 acre Black River Conservation Association with a group of friends and his son Chris. They had a small cabin on the property. Meanwhile, another son, Mark, saw an ad in the local paper about a male golden retriever puppy for sale, and he called his father about it.

"You really need another Dog, Dad."

"No," said Jerry, "I'm not interested in having another golden retriever since Old Birdie died."

"Well here's the phone number anyway, Dad. You might want to at least look at him."

When Jerry went partridge hunting that day, he mused on his friends' interactions with their bird Dogs, noticing the pleasure that the Dogs and their masters shared between each other. When he got back to his cabin, Jerry decided to call the number that Mark had given him.

The woman who answered the phone said that Jerry's son had called and thought the puppy would be perfect for his dad. When Jerry said he couldn't get out to see the Dog before Sunday on his way home from hunting, she told him that a couple of other people were interested in the puppy.

"The Dog will probably be gone by Sunday," the woman replied.

Jerry took the address, thought about the idea of another Dog and drove to the farm on Broomhead Road, between Kalkaska and Traverse City.

When he arrived, the woman greeted him while holding me in her arms. "This is Shiloh," she said. She explained how they had planned to eventually breed me with their female golden retriever, but her husband had lost his job and they needed to sell me.

As Jerry bent down toward me, I took one look at him and licked his nose. I liked the look of this man. He seemed kind, optimistic and friendly, and he smelled like sleeping bags and wood smoke. I was only three and a half months old, but I sensed that we would be an excellent fit.

Within three minutes, Jerry had written a check. (Whoever said you can't buy happiness forgot about puppies.) The woman gave him my thoroughbred papers, and before you could say "What a good deal," I was sitting next to my new master in the front seat of his Oldsmobile Bravada, riding back to the cabin.

That evening Jerry cooked for the hunters who had gathered at a cabin belonging to his friend, George. His son Chris placed me in the back seat of his car, while Jerry transported the food in the Oldsmobile. I hadn't yet learned how to control my bowels, and in my uneasiness about riding in the automobile—and without a patch of grass in sight—I pooped on Chris's car seat. He was not happy but managed to laugh about it by the time we reached George's cabin.

"Next time, we're taking your car, Pop," he said.

George didn't particularly like dogs. So when we arrived at his cabin Jerry joked, "Don't say a word, George. Shiloh stays or I don't cook."

George smiled and Jerry directed the men in the group to draw numbers. Every fifteen minutes one of them would take me out to do my business. Later on I fell asleep under the table at my new master's feet.

The next day Jerry called Barb, his wife. "Hi honey! We have a new puppy. A beautiful golden retriever named Shiloh. Yes, I know we agreed no more Dogs, and no, we won't let Shiloh interfere with our traveling. Yes, he can go to a kennel when we travel." While Jerry was talking on the phone to Barb, I had the sudden urge to do my business. I came over a couple of times, crying softly and nosing his hand, but his attention was elsewhere. I went into his bedroom and pooped right on the middle of the bed.

After the phone call ended, Jerry smelled my poop and came right into the bedroom like a homing pigeon. There it was, right on his bed. I smiled and frisked around him, trying to explain that I had tried to get his attention. He cleaned up the mess without complaint. The next day he and I drove downstate to my new home, which was south of Holland on Lake Michigan.

On the way home, Jerry visited his ninety-eight-year-old aunt Ethel in Jackson, Michigan.

She lived in an assisted living complex, and he visited her every month. He carried me into the facility and introduced me to her. Although confined to a wheelchair, she was remarkably lucid. She had been in charge of the buildings and grounds committee until she was ninety-four, when she fell and broke her hip. She asked Jerry if she could hold me in her lap. Her lap was so comfortable that I went to sleep while she stroked my head. When my master got ready to leave, Aunt Ethel said, "Be sure to bring the puppy next month." The following month everyone at the assisted living facility wanted to meet and pet me. I loved the attention.

When we got to Jerry's house and I met his wife, Barb, she petted me but said to Jerry,

"Remember, this Dog is not coming with us to Florida. He will stay in a kennel." (I am now twelve and a half years old. I have never been in a kennel, and I very much love Florida.)

Jerry began to think about having me trained as a Therapy Dog, and eventually he found a woman in Battle Creek named Sherry to train me. She was an attractive forty-year-old woman of German heritage who smelled like bacon. She ran a successful training program and bred golden retrievers. I remained with her for an entire day while she evaluated my abilities. I heard her tell my master that I would be perfect as a Therapy Dog but that I was a bit headstrong. Sherry said that she would work with me and felt that I would do well, but she wanted to evaluate Jerry to see if he would make a good master for a Therapy Dog.

After my second full day of training, Sherry asked Jerry to accompany her on a walk. She had five Dogs, including me, and none of us were on leash. She used commands such as "stay" and "sit." All of the Dogs obeyed, so I did too. It seemed appropriate to follow the behavior of the other Dogs. I had been working hard all day, so I had a good idea about what was expected of me.

I was an incredibly fast learner because golden retrievers such as myself are bred to please. I liked Sherry she was pretty in human terms, and she smelled nice. I went to Sherry's place for advanced training every week for two months.

Three months later, Jerry called Sherry and said, "I think Shiloh's progress has regressed."

The next day Jerry took me to Sherry's, and after watching us do our commands, Sherry said, "The problem is you, Jerry. You need to be the one in charge, not the Dog."

Because Sherry was having trouble with her car, Jerry drove her to her husband's office, and on the drive she observed me putting my paw on Jerry's arm. I was shocked when Sherry snapped, "Back, Shiloh."

Needless to say, I backed off, realizing that I should not have been pawing Jerry's arm while he was driving.

She turned to Jerry and said, "Never let your Dog do that." She repeated, "You are in charge, not your Dog."

I was thinking, "Sherry is still pretty but damn tough." I had learned a few swear words from my master.

When we got to her husband's office, Sherry taught Jerry about positive reinforcement training. She ordered me to stay and then walked away. I followed her. She shouted "No" emphatically and took me back to my original spot while repeating the command. I finally understood. I was not to follow her but to stay put. When I obeyed, Sherry said, "Good boy." This was an example of positive training and reinforcement.

Eventually, I earned my K-9 Good Citizen Dog Award, which allowed me to visit nursing and retirement homes. I would still require more training, however, before I could become a hospice and hospital dog. The ensuing years of my life provided much fulfillment for me and my devoted master.

CHAPTER 2

Hospet

A Dog is a comfort when you're feeling
blue because he doesn't try to find out why.

—Shiloh

I vividly remember my first experience with hospice. Barb and Jerry's friend Gary was diagnosed with cancer. We visited him at his home. When we got there, his wife, Arlene and two members of hospice were keeping Gary comfortable.

I had seen Gary before he became ill, but I could tell now that things were different for him. Although he was bedridden, his face lit up when he began to pet me. Jerry and I had picked him up months before to take him to his physical therapy. He had always been so appreciative of our support. I learned that Gary was terminally ill, and he would be making his final transition soon. The last time I saw him, I sensed that it would be the last time. Over the years I became keenly aware of my super-sniffer sense. The smell of cancer affected me so profoundly that sometimes I could hardly stay in the patient's room. This was to cause me much embarrassment in the future. One day Barb and Jerry left me at home and I later learned that they had gone to Gary's funeral.

We made several more visits to people with life-threatened illnesses. I always went to their homes and was impressed with the hospice workers' caring attitudes.

We decided to become hospice volunteers. This led to my becoming certified as a hospet to make visits both in homes and hospice facilities. I became certified first in Michigan with Therapy Dogs Inc, therapyDogsinc@qwest.net, and I received further certification in Florida. Each year Jerry has to fill out forms providing proof of my vaccinations as part of my annual recertification. I wear a special hospet scarf when I make my visits.

After we made several visits to hospice facilities, Jerry decided that we could do more good for more people by going to hospices rather than to individual homes.

In the first several months that I visited different hospice facilities, I learned three very important things: (1) to be admitted to a hospice facility, a person must have a life-threatened diagnosis; (2) patients must accept the fact that they are life-threatened and will not get better; and (3) patients' lives will not be prolonged, but they will be kept comfortable. Hospice offers a peaceful setting for those who are terminally ill and provides support for those who are left to grieve.

My hospet visits are important for the life-threatened as well as their friends and families. I also receive many pats and hugs from my favorite doctor, Roger Phillips, and other staff members at the Hospice of Holland, Michigan. We are now dividing our visits between the Hospice House in Holland from spring through fall and the Hospice Cottages at Treasure Coast Hospice of Stuart, Florida, during the winter.

People are sometimes confused about the difference between a Service Dog and a Therapy Dog. Service Dogs are trained to give assistance to the disabled, allowing their masters to function independently. They are recognized by the Americans with Disabilities Act, which gives them public access rights.

Therapy Dogs are normally registered with organizations such as Therapy Dogs Inc., and they provide a healing benefit to the general public. Most hospets are also Therapy Dogs.

CHAPTER 3

Cuba and the Navy

Castro won't last six months.

—Lt. j. g. Jerry Hill, January 1959

I n order for you to understand my role as a volunteer, you should know a little about my master's life before I became his constant companion.

Jerry was in high school during the Korean War, and his father, who was in the navy in World War I, convinced him to apply for the NROTC Program. He passed all of the tests with flying colors and signed up for twelve years in the navy. At the age of seventeen, he enrolled at the University of Michigan with substantial financial assistance from the navy program.

One of his mandatory summer cruises took him to Havana, Cuba. This was before the Cuban Revolution. Little did he realize that he would return to Cuba during the revolution for a major assignment.

After graduating from the University of Michigan, Barb and Jerry were married and went to Supply Corps School in Athens, Georgia, where Jerry received orders to relocate to Cuba. Barb was excited about visiting Havana on the weekends. Jerry didn't have the heart to tell her that from where they would be living, Havana was six hundred miles away, down narrow roads through a country in revolution. Barb never did make it to Havana.

Ensign Jerry and Barb were sent to Guantanamo Bay for three years. The way I've heard the story is that Jerry was the naval officer in charge of feeding the sailors at Guantanamo Bay. He was twenty-one years old and had 150 men working for him in a job that he knew nothing about. He worked extra hard to learn his duties. During the Cuban Revolution of the mid-1950s, providing food for the sailors was a top priority because they could seldom leave the base.

One day the Base Admiral called all of the officers together for a meeting on morale. "Anyone involved in special services, in other words, sports or food service, will have top priority for creative ideas to keep the morale up among the sailors," he said.

Jerry felt inspired and motivated, and he continually came up with creative ideas, such as making grills out of fifty-five-gallon oil drums and serving steaks cooked over charcoal. He solved the problem of getting the sailors to eat before drinking beer at the White Hat Club on paydays by serving them free submarine sandwiches and pizza. The sailors would have to carry an aluminum mess tray that they had picked up at the mess hall, and this was their ticket into the beer hall. They had to enter the front door of the mess hall, pick up a tray, and walk out the scullery door fifty feet into the White Hat Club. By walking through Jerry's mess hall front door, the master-at-arms could check each man off of a list, and Jerry's mess hall would get credit for feeding them.

The navy later investigated how Jerry's payday dinner counts averaged over 90 percent while the rest of the navy shore establishments averaged around 10 percent. After the investigation was over, Jerry received a special commendation for his ingenuity in helping the overall morale of the sailors.

However, Jerry's fondest accomplishment related to how he replaced the frozen milk (he said it was really yucky!) that was sent from the United States to Guantanamo—or Gitmo, as they called it—with fresh milk. He was told it would be impossible. It took six months for him to get past the red tape, but even then the milk was available only in Jerry's enlisted men's mess halls. Eventually Jerry arranged for fresh milk to be made available throughout the base. After the naval commissary got fresh milk, the children of service families would salute Jerry and call him Officer Milk.

All of these creative maneuvers and ideas eventually became the vanguard for Jerry's later career in the restaurant business.

CHAPTER 4

Gitmo

A puppy—a heartbeat at your feet.

—Anonymous

While living in Guantanamo Bay, Barb and Jerry received exciting news that their first child was on the way. This blessed moment brought about the planning of a flurry of activities. But even with the excitement and anticipation, something still seemed to be missing in their lives. On his way home one day, Jerry saw a sign that said "Free Puppies." Jerry took one of the puppies home and named him Gitmo. His fur was black and brown, and he was small. He was a true Heinz 57, and his addition to the family made Jerry feel that everything was complete.

At the end of the next year, Jerry received his orders to return stateside, and as a result, a Dog problem arose. There was no procedure in place for transporting a Dog from Guantanamo Bay to the States. However, Jerry had a plan. One of his storekeepers, Ski, had requested leave to visit the States over Christmas. Although Ski wasn't due for leave yet, he certainly deserved to take it. A bus had been returning him and a bunch of sailors to the base after a rare visit into Cuba, when Castro's men hijacked it. They spent three weeks in friendly captivity. Ski was a first-class petty officer and the highest ranked sailor on the fateful bus, and therefore, he represented his sailor brethren every day to either Raul or Fidel Castro. Although Ski was not permitted to talk much about his unusual absence from the base, when he was released, he was wearing a pair of Fidel's combat boots. Jerry was convinced that this was the man who could carry out the mission of smuggling his Dog Gitmo into the States.

Jerry approved Ski's leave and arranged for him to smuggle Gitmo aboard a plane that the commanding officer of the Naval Air Station would be piloting to Pensacola, Florida. When Ski arrived in Pensacola, he would send Gitmo by train to Barb's parents' home in Michigan. Even though Gitmo's kennel was discovered before take-off, he was surrounded by other contraband, including the commanding officer's golf clubs, so his presence was thankfully ignored.

Although Gitmo had experienced only hot Cuban weather, he flourished in the snowy climate of Michigan. Barb's parents reported back to Barb and Jerry in Cuba about how Gitmo would disappear for hours at a time—once he even disappeared overnight—but he always returned tired, hungry, and happy. A few months after Gitmo arrived in Michigan, a haughty standard poodle named Fife, who lived down the street, delivered a litter of very odd-looking puppies. Barb's parents described this incident as The Cuban Connection.

After Barb and Jerry's naval career ended, they returned to Michigan. Gitmo lived for more than ten years with Barb, Jerry, and their three boys, always grateful that he had escaped the world of Castro.

Maize and Blue

Happiness is a warm puppy.

—Charles M. Schulz

O ver the years, I've heard Barb tell the story about Maize and Blue. They were around before I was a part of the Hill's household and probably before I was even a glimmer in my father's eye.

To this day Barb keeps a picture of Maize and Blue on her desktop. The story goes that Barb and Jerry were living in Battle Creek when Barb saw her neighbor one day at the grocery store. The neighbor told Barb that her female toy poodle had a litter of three puppies and they were available for sale. On the way back from shopping, Barb stopped by the neighbor's house and picked out one of the female puppies and took her home. (It seems Barb and Jerry had gotten into the habit of picking up Dogs on their own without consulting each other.)

Jerry had always preferred big Dogs, and he was very uncomfortable with the tiny puppy. He did think she was cute, however. Unfortunately, the puppy cried for its entire first night at their house, and the next morning Barb and Jerry decided to return the puppy to the owner, since she had indicated that they could do so if the puppy did not work out.

"Big Dog" Jerry was nominated for the job of returning the puppy, but about an hour after he left, he returned with two puppies.

Barb was astonished. She asked, "What happened?"

Jerry explained that when he got to the puppy's house he picked up the boy puppy and the other girl puppy tried to hide behind the refrigerator. He told the owner that the puppy he took home had cried all night.

The neighbor said, "That's funny. Her sister cried all night too."

Jerry immediately put down the boy puppy and picked up the girl puppy that had cried all night and returned home with the two girl puppies.

"Big Dog" Jerry was slightly embarrassed by the two tiny puppies, but in his inimitable fashion he named them Maize and Blue, the colors of the football team of the University of Michigan, his alma mater.

Furthermore, he announced to Barb that he planned to train the puppies to push a ball from one end of a football field to the other, as another Dog had done at the Michigan stadium. "I'll teach them as soon as they are old enough to roll the ball with their noses," Jerry said.

Apparently one of the student managers trained his Dog to push a ball from one end zone to the other, before the game and during halftime. The crowds of over one hundred thousand people would go absolutely crazy cheering him on. Jerry never mentioned what breed the Dog was, but since it was smart and coordinated, I'm sure it was one of my golden ancestors.

However, Jerry, prone to exaggeration, never quite got around to fulfilling his dream of teaching the puppies to push a ball along a field. As cute as Maize and Blue were, they weren't the sharpest pups in the pack.

I've heard Barb talk about how little Maize, who was only four and a half pounds at maturity, passed away at the age of seventeen. At six pounds, Old Blue died within two weeks of Maize's passing and joined her sister in Dog heaven.

CHAPTER 6

The Career

TMI: Too Much Information

—Webster's New Dictionary

When Jerry left the navy and returned to America from Cuba, he faced a difficult decision. He could return to college to earn his Masters degree, which was confusing to me since he's always been my master; he could work in his father's wholesale automotive parts business, where he had helped out from the age of eight to seventeen; or he could accept a job with a small restaurant chain.

The owners of the restaurant were fifty-one and sixty-one years of age. They already had a great family restaurant, but expanding on their dream would require the help of two young soldiers. They had already hired a man named Dick, who had just finished his duty obligation as a Marine Quartermaster officer. Jerry had fallen in love with food and service as a Navy Supply Corps officer, so he signed on. For the two restaurant founders, their war had been won.

He continued working for exactly thirty-three and one-third years to the day, and after working at every job in the business, he worked his way up to the positions of President, CEO, and Vice Chairman of the Board.

My master experienced a remarkable career. His career would make a very interesting story. However, this is the story of my life. But I will share a few of his retirement stories, as they are very worthy of being told. They seem to best explain his spirit of adventure, intrigue, and suspense. Having come into his life at a later stage, his career and retirement adventures were what shaped him into the man whom I know and love today.

CHAPTER 7

The Retiree

*How old would you be if you
didn't know how old you are?*

—Unknown

I've heard this story several times, so I assume it's true. My master retired at the age of fifty-eight. His business partner and Barb protested against this decision, but Jerry's reasoning won out. He loved his career, but the energy that was required to run a successful restaurant business, opening sixty-five new locations and catering to the needs of four thousand employees, was beginning to take its toll.

Two meaningful events reinforced Jerry's desire to leave work behind: his older brother had narrowly escaped death through a successful heart transplant and his first grandchild was born.

He worked for long hours, traveling regularly between all of the restaurants in five states, and he had a long bucket list to get started on.

Three suitcases were packed and ready for the start of Jerry's retirement, the Big R. The first trip he took was to Canada to fish with a bunch of his friends. Next came a two-week visit to Alaska with Barb. Jerry loved Alaska and later returned on two more fishing trips.

Another trip, however, proved to be the most interesting. Jerry and his good friend, Bud, went to Las Vegas. As they lay in the scalding sun by the old MGM pool, Bud asked, "Who's that guy over there by the tennis house?"

Jerry said, "That's Jimmy Connors."

"No, Jimmy Connors is bigger than that," Bud insisted. "I'll bet you ten bucks it's Connors."

"Make it twenty and you're on," Bud said, sure of himself.

As Jerry approached, Jim Connors was winding up a conversation with a young woman named Mary. Jerry said, "Hey Jimmy, how you doing?"

"Great. Good to see you." He shook hands with Jerry and left.

Mary asked, "You a friend of Jimmy's?"

"Yup," Jerry responded.

To Jerry's complete surprise, Mary scheduled him for the next morning to play a game of tennis with Connors at the Desert Inn in the Cancer Crusade Fundraiser. My master hurried back to tell Bud about his good fortune and collect his twenty-dollar bet.

"I have to shop to buy everything I will need for the game," Jerry said, "but let's get a bite to eat first."

Bud thought that Jerry had fabricated the entire story to separate Bud from his money, but he went along with Jerry to the poolside snack bar anyway. They picked up a couple of hot Dogs and drinks, and sat at the only table available. Within a few moments, Mary appeared with Jimmy Connors and two other women.

"Can we share your table?" Mary asked.

"Of course," Jerry said.

"This is Patti Connors and Gloria Connors," said Mary, referring to the women with Jimmy.

Bud's jaw dropped as he looked at Jerry with a conceding expression.

Jerry and Bud finished their food, said their goodbyes, and took a cab to shop for tennis equipment.

The next day, Connors let Jerry win one of the three games they played. One year later, due to a freak meeting in Las Vegas with a man named Mr. Agassi, Jerry played again in the cancer fundraiser against Agassi's eight-year-old son, Andre. My master played hard to win one game out of three against Andre, who wasn't as generous as Connors had been the previous year.

A year later, Jerry traveled to a tennis camp at Palmetto Dunes on Hilton Head Island, South Carolina, and as one of two top-rated amateur players, he played against resident professional Rod Laver and a third amateur in a one-set exhibition. Much to everyone's surprise, Jerry and his partner won with a score of 6–2.

These events spotlight how Jerry is one of the few amateur tennis players to win at least one game from three different Wimbledon Champions: Connors, Agassi, and Laver.

While Jerry does tend to exaggerate, I do believe that this really happened. These events give you a glimpse into how lucky my master was and is. After all, he has me, right?

CHAPTER 8

Meeting Kate

There is no better feeling in the world than
a puppy licking your face.

—Kate

When I was almost six-months old, Jerry announced, "The fall colors are at their peak and we're going north to enjoy them. We'll all stay at the cabin."

It was my second cabin visit since I had been in Jerry's life.

When we arrived, two of his granddaughters, Carly who was six years old and Lindsay who was five, were there. They were the daughters of Jerry's son Mark and his wife Anne. I ran around the cabin, both inside and outside, while the girls chased but never caught me.

Later on, Tim and Char arrived in their car, along with their young daughter Kate. After greeting everyone,

Tim carried Kate inside. Someone opened the cabin door and I went inside to run and play some more. I soon realized there was this little girl crawling on the floor. I liked her looks because she was so tiny. I don't know why, but I dropped on all fours and began crawling toward her. She headed toward me and we met nose to nose. I licked her on the nose, and she instantly licked me back on my nose. Laughter arose from all parts of the room. Later I learned that Kate had Down syndrome and that her mother Char was a very fastidious person, so licking noses probably wasn't on her normal radar. I'm glad we licked noses, though because it helped Kate and me enter into a very special relationship.

Children with Down syndrome do very well when given the chance, and they have made significant contributions to the world. By observing these special children, we can all learn about forgiveness and unconditional love.

Oxytocin is the name of the love potion that surges through my body when people are kind to me and pet me. I love getting attention, and I wish I could pass this special feeling onto all children with Down syndrome. No one loved is ever lost and the love that people give to these children is returned unconditionally tenfold.

I also learned that Dogs often suffer abuse and neglect. Many years ago Dogs were sometimes treated like slaves, and they were beaten when they misbehaved or didn't fulfill their master's expectations. I'm thankful that I was born after organizations such as People for the Ethical Treatment of Animals (PETA) and others of good conscience virtually put a stop to such practices.

Let's hope and pray that animals and humans alike who are forced to endure wrongful hardships will find peace and happiness.

CHAPTER 9

Twin Birch

If your Dog is fat,
you're not getting enough exercise.

—Anonymous

A week after we left the cabin outside of Traverse City to go downstate, we were driving north again toward the hunting cabin. When we passed the front gate, Jerry explained, "Shiloh, we're going to Twin Birch and you're going to see your hero, Mark."

None of this made sense to me, until we pulled into the parking lot of the Twin Birch Golf Course and I spotted Jerry's oldest son Mark, the one who had initially brought me to Jerry's attention. I remember vividly when he came to the house on Broomhead Road, picked me up, and told the lady of the house, "I'm calling my dad. This puppy is perfect for him." And I was perfect for him.

I wasn't the only one who thought of Mark as my hero. He was a professional golfer for the PGA, and he had purchased this golf course, with the help of the bank, earlier that year.

Mark was a fun guy, and after Jerry updated him about how well I had been adapting to my new life, Mark exclaimed, "Shiloh, you're going for a fast run."

Almost immediately, I found myself running alongside Mark's golf cart as he drove around his golf course, planning his late fall close-up.

Suddenly, I left the side of Mark's cart. Something mysterious and unfamiliar appeared before my eyes: a flock of wild turkeys. Mark cut off my adventure, however, by driving the cart between the turkeys and me.

Mark jumped off the cart, hoisted me into his strong arms, and positioned me on the seat next to him.

"Shiloh, it's a good thing it was turkeys you were chasing and not the bobcat that has its lair in the woods behind the seventeenth green," Mark said with a grin.

When we passed the seventeenth green, he laughed again. "Bob must be sleeping. Lucky for you, he's mostly nocturnal." Soon we were on the eighteenth tee and Mark explained, "Look, Shiloh, in the middle of the fairway those two birches give the course its name." Later, I learned that very few golfers could hit their tee shots past the birches. However, Mark could do it consistently, and he usually hit his second shot onto the par five, eighteenth green. In golfing terms, this meant that he would be putting for an eagle. Early in my life, I was confused about golfing terms such as *eagles* and *birdies*, and I grew even more confused when I learned that Mark had a Dog named Birdie.

I never ran into Bob, the resident bobcat at Twin Birch, but I did hear about occasional bobcat sightings among the golfers.

Unfortunately, ten years later, as the national and state economies deteriorated, Twin Birch was foreclosed. During this period, I listened while Mark and Jerry attempted to get help from the government's so-called help programs. However, these programs were mainly designed to attract new start-up businesses, at the expense of many established small businesses in America. Jerry complained about the politics of the situation, saying that there was too much red tape to deal with, but this was a subject that I knew nothing about.

CHAPTER 10

Birdie and Mark

*Almost everyone was eager to make friends
with me and I felt the same toward them.*

—Birdie

Early in his golfing career, Mark was an assistant
professional at a northern Michigan golf course for
five months out of the year. He would drive to West
Palm Beach, Florida, for the other seven months, where he
played on a mini-tour and worked part-time at a golf course.

In the summer of 1982, Mark was working in northern
Michigan when he got a golden retriever puppy and named
him Birdie. When I first heard this story, I thought, "Why
wouldn't a golf pro name his Dog, Eagle?" Later, as I got to
know Mark better, I realized that he was a great golfer, but
he was no braggart. Also, I heard about his friend, Jack, an
amateur golfer who named his Dog Bogey. (I've yet to meet
a Dog named Par.)

For the next eight years, Mark and Birdie drove back and forth between Michigan and Florida, with Birdie riding in the passenger seat.

In 1990, way before my time, Mark stopped with Birdie for a few days in Battle Creek to visit his mom and dad on his way to Florida.

He announced to Jerry and Barb, "I have a problem. My condo in West Palm no longer allows big Dogs. I'm sure I can work it out, so I've purchased a sky kennel. Please ship him to me as soon as I call to say it's okay."

Mark couldn't get his condo to change their rules, so he never made the call. Birdie and Jerry, then, bonded over the next eight years.

The stories about Birdie were legendary, and I was intrigued every time I heard Mark, Barb, and Jerry tell them. Birdie seemed to have a rogue streak in him that led him to many adventures. My favorite story involved Mark taking the job as head pro at a country club in Ishpeming, Michigan, in the Upper Peninsula. Five miles from his pro shop, he rented a cottage on a lake surrounded by woods. Every day, Birdie would go for a swim on his own after Mark had left for work. In the late morning, Birdie would appear at the golf course exhausted and covered in burrs, and Mark would patiently comb his coat back to its normal condition.

One day Birdie didn't show up, and he was gone for four days. Among the wolves, bears, coyotes, and skunks of the north woods, Mark wondered if Birdie would be able to survive. He somehow managed to make it back alive, and on the fourth day, Mark found him lying on the doorstep of the cottage when he arrived home. That must have been quite the reunion.

The next day, Mark left Birdie in the cottage. When he returned home to let him out, Birdie made a beeline for the neighbor's grill and pulled the half-cooked steak off and brought it to Mark as a peace offering. Mark loved Birdie, so he reluctantly accepted the gift. He then headed to his neighbor's home with wallet in hand, to apologize and repay him for the pilfered steak.

After Birdie came to live with Barb and Jerry, their good friends, Keith and Doris, arrived from Florida. Everyone went out except for Keith, whom Jerry had asked to walk Birdie on his leash. I've actually heard Keith tell this story.

"We were walking, when a huge German shepherd named Sarge appeared. Birdie had just finished his *drip-till-you-drop* routine for the umpteenth time, and unfortunately he had sprayed some of his marking fluid onto Sarge's lawn. Birdie was crafty and old, while Sarge was tough and bold, and a fight ensued." Keith continued, "I never realized an old seventy-five pound Dog could pull so hard, and down I went with these two animals fighting inches away. Thankfully, a loud voice belted out, 'Sarge, *no!*' and the fracas ended. It was then that I met Sarge's master, an ex-marine, and I fully understood the connection between the Dog's name and its demeanor."

Birdie died on June 4, 1998, at the age of sixteen. Jerry and Mark were both heartbroken. When Mark married, he and his wife acquired a sheltie puppy, but Barb and Jerry agreed that they did not want to get another Dog. That agreement clearly didn't hold up, because I became a member of their family. Amazingly, I was born on the exact day that old Birdie had passed on. Is it possible that I'm his reincarnation? Who knows?

CHAPTER 11

Hunting

Hunting Dogs and their trainers:
poetry in motion

—Tim Hill

At sixteen months old, I was fully grown and I had lived with Jerry and Barb for over a year. When I first arrived in their lives, Jerry and I spent a lot of time at their cabin in the north woods. I was looking forward to September 15, the opening of small game season, because this entailed packing up the Bravada and heading north to the woods. I had learned that the beloved cabin was originally built in 1924, out of cedar logs harvested from a nearby swampy area. It was primitive but cozy.

I had spent much of the spring and summer volunteering as a Therapy Dog. I will tell you a little bit about my hunting experiences, but I promise to share my therapy experiences later on.

Hunting is a sport, and although hunters hunt for game, hunting is not a game. When people hunt, they step into a special world that is wild and natural, and it's important that all hunters respect this special world. I was privileged enough to go on a lot of bird and deer hunts.

Jerry taught his three sons the same things about hunting that his dad taught him: treat every gun like it's loaded even when you know it's not, never aim your gun at any animal that you don't intend to shoot, and never shoot anything that you don't plan to eat. Good hunters are usually good people. I've learned a lot through my master and through my personal observations around the hunting camp.

In autumn, folks from downstate drive to northern Michigan for color tours of the autumn foliage. I remember those perfect autumn days with a chill in the air and tree leaves blazing orange, red, and yellow everywhere in the hardwood forest. The brilliant colors painted a glorious scene against the dark, textured trunks of the trees and the smooth carpet of leaves on the forest floor.

Sometimes after dinner, Jerry's son, Tim, and his buddy, Larry, would play their favorite song on dueling guitars. Readers, I want you to know that what happens in deer camp stays in deer camp. Tim and Larry often sang the following song after having imbibed a few adult beverages. They were having fun with the lyrics, and they didn't really believe the things they were singing about. As you will see, they were not quite ready for any sort of prime time performance. Their song went like this:

This is my land,
It's not your land,

I've got a shotgun
And you ain't got one.
Off this land you'd better git,
'Fore my shotgun hits ya where ya sit,
'Cause this land belongs to only me.

While this song is not serious, I know that Jerry's friends really do love their land.

This purpose of the trip was to hunt for birds, such as partridge (ruffed grouse) and woodcock. In the hunter's lingo it's Pats (Partridge) and Timberdoodles (Woodcock). I never understood the word *Timberdoodles* until I first heard one flush and fly. I thought to myself, "Wow! What a lot of noise that bird can make."

We hunted with shorthaired, German pointers that belonged to some friends. These Dogs were experienced, so I stayed behind my master and observed. When a partridge or woodcock was shot, the hunter would command his Dog to "bird down" and "fetch." I was amazed at their ability to locate the downed bird and retrieve it for their masters. My natural hunting instincts took over and I wanted in on the hunt.

A few days later, my wish came true when the other hunters had left for home, leaving my master and me alone on the land. While driving in the old Army surplus jeep, he suddenly stopped and commanded me to stay. I couldn't see any birds as he quietly left the jeep, removed his 20-gauge over-and-under Browning Citori shotgun from its case, loaded in two shells, and quietly walked off. I had watched him clean his gun back at the cabin on occasion, and I was intrigued about the gold-plated engraving of a flying bird and a golden retriever on the side of the shotgun.

Jerry returned quickly. I had heard two shots, and I had my hopes up about joining him. My hopes were fulfilled when he said with a huge smile, "Come Shiloh, we're going to test your hunting instincts."

I had never received any formal training for hunting birds, but I have always been a quick learner. When my master pointed toward the woods and said, "Fetch, Shiloh," I dashed into the area he had indicated. I gently picked up the first partridge of my career and proudly sat in front of my master with the bird in my mouth. When he said, "Good boy, Shiloh. Drop," I released the prize and offered my paw to him.

Jerry laughed and shook my paw. He said, "Congratulations, Bird Dog. Now, Shiloh, fetch." He pointed to another area of the woods, and I charged back into the brush. I located my second bird, or pat, easily. As I'm now a successful, experienced retrieving bird Dog, I can refer to the bird as a pat, but during my first hunt, I was still young and full of vigor. I started throwing my second fetch bird into the air and catching it repeatedly. A rather stern Jerry spoke words I've seldom heard when he said, "No, Shiloh. No!"

With this reprimand, I returned to Jerry without the bird. Jerry simply said, "Shiloh, fetch!" In a microsecond I was back in the brush and returned proudly with the second bird. Instead of waiting for his command, I dropped the bird at Jerry's feet. He reached down to pet and hug me and said, "Good Boy, Shiloh. You're the best." I liked that praise a lot, especially when it came from my master.

Jerry field-dressed the birds by placing his hunting boots on each wing and pulling upward on the bird's feet. This separated the breast from the remainder of the bird. He then examined the crop of each bird to see what they had been eating. He found each bird had been feeding upon wintergreen leaves, berries and beechnuts.

That evening Jerry prepared one of the breasts with garlic, butter, seasonings, and wine. He put the other breast in the freezer to save it for some hunters arriving at a later date. The smell was awesome, however Jerry explained, "Sorry, pup, can't let you lick the old iron skillet with all that garlic."

I ate my regular dinner and took a walk with Jerry around the triangle, a one-mile route that starts and ends at the cabin. I jumped onto someone's sleeping bag on an open bed, and I was fast asleep in seconds, having wonderful hunting dreams about fetching a covey of pats and laying them at Jerry's feet.

CHAPTER 12

Carol and the Cat

*If you can look at a Dog and not feel
vicarious excitement and affection,
you must be a cat.*

—Anonymous

After a while, Jerry began to feel uneasy and guilty about goofing off at the north woods cabin. It was nice to sleep in, drive around seventeen miles of two-track dirt roads while looking for wildlife, take long walks and hunt for partridge and woodcock, but something was missing. I myself didn't feel guilty, because sleeping, riding in the jeep and hunting were all at the top of my to-do list.

One day my master said, "Shiloh, we can't get lazy and complacent. We're going to the hospital in Kalkaska." I couldn't figure out how laziness and complacency would land us in the hospital, but I went along. It turned out that we were going to provide therapy for those in need.

When we met Carol, who was to be our tour guide and nurse we bonded with her instantly. With blonde hair and big blue eyes, Carol was a lovely woman, and I loved the way she stroked my head and gently petted me with her soft hands.

Almost immediately, I came nose-to-nose with a resident cat. We looked each other in the eyes and for one moment we remained quite still. I was sizing him up and he was probably doing the same. He had shiny black fur and large green eyes with which he dared to provoke me. Suddenly, he turned and darted down the hallway and the chase was on. I was right behind him. We took a left turn and swooped past a man on a bed who rose up and watched us race by.

"I'll put a fiver on the cat," he hollered to anyone who might be taking bets.

Another man walked to the doorway of his room as I was gaining on the cat and said, "I'll wager a ten spot on the Dog. He's bigger."

The cat made a right turn, and I ran straight into a staff person's legs, nearly knocking him off his feet. Next, we charged past a patient who was walking, narrowly missing him. Then we ran down another hallway. Just as I was overtaking the cat, he spun under a cart and I ran into some equipment, which tumbled to the floor. Ink Spot, as the cat was named, swooped through a doorway that had been propped open. I realized that the door wasn't open far enough for me to follow, so I skidded to a halt and regretfully lost the race.

When Jerry and Carol caught up with me, she suggested that I leave. I was disappointed that I couldn't stay to run another race with Ink Spot. I hoped that I could catch him next time, but there was to be no next time. I was banished from the hospital. I did want to get to know Carol better, but that wasn't to happen either. She was very pretty and smelled good like powder and perfume. Her human aroma overrode the normal hospital smells and I imagined being with her in a deer blind, which would have been a vast improvement over being in one with Jerry.

Thankfully, Carol wasn't angry with me. She said, "It wasn't your fault, Shiloh. I should have alerted you about our resident cat."

However, that wouldn't have made any difference. I still would have chased Ink Spot. I love to chase cats; it's part of my job in life.

I was falling in love and Jerry sensed my attraction to Carol. As I reluctantly left, Carol suggested that we visit the nearby senior center. I never saw Carol again, but I've never forgotten her.

CHAPTER 13

Rita

Remember that silence is sometimes the best answer.

—The Dalai Lama

When we arrived at the senior center, the beautiful Carol had already called to tell them about my Therapy Dog credentials. A nice lady by the name of Dolores informed us that today was one of the three days out of the week when mentally challenged adults came to the center.

Dolores introduced us to eight of these adults, who were sitting in a large room with lots of windows. She called each person by name until she came to a petite woman named Rita, who was blind and very timid. She never spoke and no one knew whether she was capable of speaking.

Dolores introduced me flatteringly to Rita, describing me as a beautiful golden retriever. I prefer to be called handsome, but I accepted beautiful.

Rita became suddenly agitated, so we moved away from her and attended to the other people in the room. Big John was one person I wanted to stay away from because he loved to tackle me and roll me over. I played dead and that slowed him down somewhat. On subsequent visits, when Big John repeated his roughhouse tactics, I would sometimes wish that I wasn't a therapy Dog so that I could give him a nip or two. On one visit, when the same eight people were seated around a table working with their hands, I tried to avoid Big John by going to Rita's side of the table. They usually ate lunch before we arrived, and I hoped that maybe Rita had dropped some food next to her chair. In my haste to find some morsels on the floor, I brushed against Rita's hand. She leaned over and reached for me. I licked her hand, thinking that I smelled food on it. She immediately began to cry. I felt horrible; I hadn't meant to make her cry. My master came over to the table and apologized to Rita, but she began to talk non-stop as she again reached for me.

"Rita happy. Rita loves Shalow," she repeated over and over as she ran her hand through my coat. I remained motionless for a long time under Rita's caring hands.

When it was time to leave, we learned that Rita had been coming to the center for two years and had never spoken a word until she spoke to me.

For the next two years, during hunting season, we returned to the center to visit Rita and the others. Rita continued a non-stop conversation with me, and continued to call me Shalow.

One time when we returned to the center, a staff person met us at the door and explained that they now had a new client who was allergic to Dog hair.

I felt terrible that I wouldn't be able to wrestle with Big John or bring my unconditional love to Rita anymore. While we did attempt to visit once when the allergic person wasn't there, we weren't successful. I never knew what it meant to be allergic to dog hair, and the worst part about the whole situation was that I never saw Rita again. I heard Jerry tell other people about how much I meant to Rita and how I had helped her reacquire the ability to talk. That alone made being a Therapy Dog worthwhile.

I felt good about volunteering in Kalkaska and I found it hard to go back downstate at the time of year when the north woods are the most beautiful. However, I was happy to see Barb. With lots of laughter and petting, she reassured me, "Shiloh, you'll be headed back north in a few weeks." And she was right.

CHAPTER 14
Beaver Dam ‑Damn Beavers

When man is in trouble, God sends him a Dog.—<u>Alphonse De Lamartine</u> *When Dog is in trouble, God sends him a man.*

—Shiloh

We headed back north to my favorite place: the cabin, deep in the woods. It was Veterans Day, November 11, and Jerry told me that I was now a veteran of two bird seasons and one deer season, so I qualified to be honored on this day. Of course, I understood that Veterans Day was really a celebration for all our servicemen like my master, but I did like his analogy.

If I were good, he told me that he'd take me out into his deer blind that year and this really excited me.

When we arrived at the cabin, Jerry built a fire in the fireplace, placed the screen in front of it, and off we went with about an hour or two of daylight left.

"Time for a hunting walk, Shiloh," Jerry said.

We went out to an area we called the Triangle, both of us on the lookout for birds. My master carried his favorite Citori shotgun. Halfway into the one-mile walk, a storm front suddenly hit, bringing high winds and flurries of snow. I could hardly see the path in front of me, so my nose became our main navigational device. We continued along the two-track road and headed back to the cabin.

Suddenly, out of the swirling snow, three whitetail deer exploded across our trail, passing within twenty-five feet of us. With the snow intensifying, I could barely see them, but my natural instincts overcame my better judgment. I raced off toward the deer as Jerry froze in his tracks. "Shiloh, No!" he yelled. I was nearly out of earshot and I hate to admit it, but I blew off his command. I'm sure he followed with, "Shiloh, come," but by this time I couldn't hear him.

I was on a mission and I was convinced that I was closing the distance between the whitetails and myself. It was amazing how the deer ran between the trees in the driving snowstorm. I was sure that I saw antlers on the third deer. Traversing his rack between these trees must have been a big challenge. I didn't know how far I had run, but I guessed it had been about a mile. The snow was so thick that I could barely see the deer jump across a meandering creek. All I could hear was the wind in my ears and the pounding of my heart as I continued on my quest. As I approached the creek, it looked quite wide, with deadfall logs strewn across it. I slowed down and walked carefully across the log jam. Then came the worst moment of my life. I fell through a hole in the log jam. Little did I know that it was really a beaver dam. I had never seen a beaver or a dam, nor had I heard any of the hunters talk about them.

I found myself immersed in a gaping hole at the top of the beaver dam. As I fell, I instinctively extended my paws out to stop my fall. I found myself submerged in the water, with only my front paws and head above the level of the dam. My back paws and my hindquarters were dangling in the ice-cold, rushing water and I feared that if I let go with my front paws my entire body would be underwater in a cave-like prison. Although I was a good swimmer in Lake Michigan, I knew that I wouldn't have a chance underwater here. With the wind rushing past my head, I tried yelping a few times, but my sounds didn't carry for more than a few feet. I was terrified that I would never do therapy work again or run along the Lake Michigan shore. Most of all, I regretted that I might never be able to sleep on my master's bed or feel his tender touch again.

My front paws were aching from the pressure of holding my entire body upright. I began to drift in and out of consciousness. My thoughts flashed to a time when I was a small puppy. I had just met Jerry and I was licking his nose as he held me in his lap and brushed my coat.

Reality set in as I heard Jerry's voice calling to me through the forest, "Shiloh, Shiloh, come!" With all the strength I had left, I yelped and within minutes Jerry was crawling out onto the beaver dam. His hunting cap was covered with snow, his face was cold and wet and his eyes were wide with fear. I had never seen that look in his eyes before. He kept saying, "Shiloh, stay." I obeyed because I didn't want to go anywhere except out of this dreaded hole.

Jerry finally reached me. Lying prone on the beaver dam, he tried pulling me up by my collar and muzzle, but he couldn't get any leverage because I weighed over seventy pounds. He stood up with great difficulty and super-human effort. He reached down and pulled me by my front shoulders straight up and out of the hole. Then suddenly he lost his balance and fell backwards into the creek. I fell on top of him and realized that things had gotten worse. Fortunately, the dammed-up creek was only four feet deep at that point. Jerry pulled me to the edge of the creek and within seconds we were lying side-by-side in the deepening snow. For a while I wasn't sure that we were capable of moving, but a great inner strength came to us as we struggled to get upright and headed back to the cabin. Much to our horror, Jerry's tracks had quickly filled in with the drifting snow. Later, I heard Jerry say that this had been the only time he had been in the woods without a compass in his pocket. He had to guess which path to take to return to the Triangle road to the cabin. We were traversing a swampy area and it was difficult to walk and make any progress. I wasn't able to walk straight because I was in shock. My master reached down and guided me by my collar as we made our way through the swamp, at times nearly crawling. Finally we reached higher ground. Jerry dragged me for almost an hour until we stumbled and collapsed onto the two-track road. It was pitch dark by now. I could feel the snow in my face and an ache in my hindquarters. However, I had complete confidence that my master would find our way home. He couldn't drag me anymore, so he commanded me to stay and he left me. I was cold, hurting and scared. I must have fallen asleep for a while.

I began to dream that I was a bad little bear who had run away from home, and this dream was probably inspired by a story that had been told at one of the pre-school reading groups where Jerry and I volunteered. The little bear had been bad and his mama and papa bear were very upset with him. He decided to run away from home. When it started snowing again, I sat on the side of the road and cried. Then car lights appeared through the snow and what I imagined to be a papa bear got out of the Jeep. In reality, it was really Jerry. He picked me up and placed me gently in the back seat.

He said, "I'm sorry, pup, that I left you. It was the only chance to get you back to the warmth of the cabin as quickly as possible."

Within minutes he was carrying me into the cabin, where he laid me in front of a roaring fire, which he had built hurriedly from the embers of the earlier fire. He had called a vet, who told him, "You must rub Shiloh with towels for his circulation to come back and prevent frostbite and hypothermia." He started rubbing me with towels. Frozen fur and ice were deeply embedded in my coat and it took Jerry a long time rubbing me to get me dry.

My master gave me a mixed concoction of warm milk and whiskey to lap up. He had to put it between my paws, as I was unable to stand up. He also poured himself a scotch and sat next to me. The scotch and whiskey were Jerry's idea and not the vet's. Although the fire was incredibly hot, he partially leaned over me and fell asleep. He was shivering almost uncontrollably. I nudged him and licked his face until he became conscious. He then stripped off all of his wet, frozen clothes and took a long, hot shower. Once he was dressed, he made a second drink for each of us and sat on the floor with his arm around me, staring into the fire.

He was talking out loud, and as I drifted into sleep, the last thing I remember him muttering was, "Damn beavers!"

I must have slept for over twelve hours, because when I woke up, the daylight was streaming through the cabin window. Jerry was asleep on the floor. Though the fire had burned out, the cabin was warm and cozy because Jerry had turned on the space heater.

Struggling to even stand up, I staggered past my empty food dish and went straight to my water bowl. I drank it dry and pushed it over the kitchen floor, making enough noise to wake Jerry from his slumber. He yawned and told me he had a beaver hangover. I could identify with that, as I felt out of sorts myself. However, all of my body parts were working again, and for that I was thankful.

We took it easy all day and fell into a more normal sleep. The next day other deer hunters began to arrive, and the day after that, November 13, all three of Jerry's sons arrived to celebrate his birthday. At the birthday celebration, there was lots of food and drinks, and many stories were told. I lay under the dining table in my usual spot and was frightened all over again as I heard my rescuer describe our beaver dam debacle. It was especially frightening when Jerry said, "I didn't think I could pull him out of the hole. God helped give me the strength I needed to do it." It was equally frightening when I heard him recount our adventure, saying, "When we both fell into the water, I thought my head hit something and I temporally blacked out. The cold water must have revived me because the next thing I remember, we were both on the bank. I still can't remember how we got there."

One of Jerry's sons said, "Dad, it's your birthday. Have another drink."

"How about me," I thought to myself. "Milk and whiskey, please." No one jumped up to fix me a drink, so I fell asleep again.

The following day more hunters arrived, yet nobody said anything about me going with Jerry to his deer blind for the opening day of deer season. Two days later, after spending most of the days by myself in the cabin, my hope was realized, and I found myself in Jerry's deer blind. It was my second year at deer camp but my first opportunity to join the hunt and I was elated.

I would lie near Jerry's feet and look between the deadfall and the logs for the brown patches of animals to appear. Whenever I saw something and tried to make eye contact with Jerry to alert him, he would already be zeroed in on the animal. He would only shoot if it was a large buck, six points or larger, and a high percentage shot. I had heard the story of how at the age of fourteen, Jerry shot his first buck at seventy-five yards, with an 1894 model Winchester 30-30 rifle, the gun that won the West. This later fact, I learned while watching old cowboy movies on TV. He was the only member of the Conservation Club, where the cabin was located, who had won the Big Buck trophy more than five times. He had won it nine times in total, and considering there were about thirty members hunting every season, that was quite remarkable.

That evening I slept soundly and my dreams were filled with visions of big bucks. The freezing water of the creek and the damn beaver dam receded in my memory as incidents often do when they fade further into the past.

Another story I loved to hear was about how Jerry's good buddy, George, had won the trophy twice in the early 1960s, before Jerry had won it for his first time. Around 1965, George shot a ten-point buck and he was ecstatic. Although it had never happened before, a member who won the trophy three times would receive a permanent facsimile retired trophy. George felt that he was on the verge of immortality because nobody in the club had ever killed a deer larger than a ten-point buck. He was confident his buck would be the winner. George celebrated his coming stardom by drinking...a lot. After four days of prematurely celebrating, a member named Bob knocked on the cabin door and asked for help in hanging his buck in the shed, where everyone brought their bucks to be weighed and hung before they left camp.

After several of the hunters helped Bob out, one of them roused George from his self-imposed stupor and said, "George, there's something you ought to know. You are no longer the buck leader in the Clubhouse. Bob's buck is a twelve-pointer." George could only say, "No, no, no, no." He then returned to his drinking, and this time it was for an entirely different reason.

The years passed and George's good friend, Jerry, won the trophy nine times before George finally won it for a third time. Although this is the same George I mentioned earlier, the one who doesn't like Dogs, I still feel badly for him whenever I hear that story.

CHAPTER 15

Slide Shiloh, Slide

There is telepathy between myself and Jerry,
a powerful factor into understanding each other.

—Shiloh

The following summer I went to my first Buddy Walk for the Down Syndrome Association, where I walked with my special pal, Kate, and many other children and young adults with Down syndrome. After one trip around the park, the adults went to the picnic area to prepare lunch, and I went with the kids to the playground, where there were swings, monkey bars, teeter-totters and a slide.

After watching for a while and being petted and hugged by several kids, a boy, John, approached Jerry and said, "Have Shiloh go up and slide down the slide."

Jerry told the boy, "Shiloh will go up but he doesn't know how to slide down."

I went up the slide's wide steps and sat at the top next to Kate, Jerry's granddaughter, who kept sliding down and returning back to the top. John started goading me into sliding. I was somewhat confused, so I stayed put. The strange surroundings were making me nervous, but my master's strong voice calmed me down.

Jerry's patience had been worn thin from John's constant chatter. He stood at the bottom of the slide, looked at me, and in a very loud voice said, "Slide, Shiloh, Slide." Then, in almost a whisper, he said, "Shiloh, Come." Although the word *slide* meant nothing to me, I responded to his second command and started to walk down the slide. Suddenly my hind legs slipped on the polished metal surface and I was on my butt sliding down, just as John had wanted. When I reached the bottom of my inaugural slide, I began to run and a bunch of kids followed behind me. Eventually, Jerry called me back to the slide, and I went up and down it many times. Word quickly spread and soon a swarm of children were waiting for me at the bottom. I hit the ground and ran some figure eights, becoming the Buddy Walk's first entertainer. John was proud of me, and he told Jerry, "See, Shiloh slides!"

Kate's mother, Char, took over the Down Syndrome Association of Western Michigan with help from her husband, Tim. My first Buddy Walk included less than one hundred kids, friends and adults. Ten years later this same event attracted more than fifteen hundred people.

Kate is very lucky to have such great and caring parents, and Char and Tim are lucky to have such a special daughter. I feel lucky too, as the association has pretty much adopted me as their poster Dog. Every year I get to walk with Kate at the very front of the Buddy Walk.

The Down Syndrome Association, or DSA, has some awesome fund-raisers, including golf outings. But the one that I really want to crash is the annual biggie, which is held at a prestigious country club where the participants watch the Kentucky Derby horse race and have a spectacular dinner. So far, the closest I've gotten to an event like this is watching the movie *Sea Biscuit* on TV. I'm still trying to work my way into the auction, where the highest bidder would walk me around the dining room winner's circle, just like the derby winner at Churchill Downs.

CHAPTER 16

My Friend Dekeon

The most affectionate creature in the world is a wet Dog.

—Ambrose Bierce

I was two years old when I first met Dekeon. Though I'm not sure what breed he was, I know that he was a pointer because wherever he pointed his nose was the direction that he and I would go in. He lived with Johnny, who was the son of a neighbor. Johnny had a mobile Dog-grooming van and would come to people's homes to groom their Dog. Since we had already met Mary at Dogs by Design, we stayed loyal to her for all of our grooming needs. Johnny, Jerry, Dekeon and I all became fast friends. And I mean *fast*. Dekeon had to be the fastest Dog that wasn't a greyhound. I don't support Dog races, so I've never actually seen a greyhound run, but I've heard stories about how fast they are.

When I turned three years old, on June 4, 2001, I was taking a swim in Lake Michigan when a bolt of lightning named Dekeon charged through the surf and swam toward me. We exited the big lake and hit the beach for some serious sniffing and running. Within seconds we were in front of Johnny's folk's home and there was Johnny with his big smile saying, "Shiloh, does Jerry know where you are?" I hadn't thought much about it, but Johnny suggested that I head home. He pointed south on the beach and I headed up the wrong set of steps, with Dekeon right behind me. Then I heard Jerry's familiar voice calling," Shiloh, come." I headed across a couple of neighbors' lawns, pausing to take a quick whiz, which Dekeon matched, and then we were on our front deck with Jerry. We heard Johnny calling, "Dekeon, Come," and off he went. Jerry told me to stay and then said, "on heel," and we went down the sixty-one steps to chat with Johnny and Dekeon on the beach.

Johnny exclaimed, "Dekeon's got extra energy today because it's his birthday." At that point the four of us realized for the first time that Dekeon and I were born on the exact same day. This cemented our relationship even more and anytime Johnny was at his parent's house, he would call Jerry and the four of us would meet on the beach.

On one of these days with Johnny and Dekeon, Jerry demonstrated our own automatic Dog washing system. He threw a stick into the lake and I retrieved it, and as soon as I hit the sandy beach, Jerry was waiting there with the Dog shampoo. My favorite shampoo was oatmeal scented. He threw another stick into the turf, where I got rinsed off before returning to him, ready for the conditioner. After chasing another stick into the water and rinsing off again,

I was ready to go to the dunes to roll around in the grass. By this time, Jerry and Johnny were sitting in sand chairs, drinking beers. After another run with Dekeon, I laid down next to Jerry. Eventually, when Jerry woke me from what he called my "Jonathon Livingston Seagull dream," I was almost dry, and I noticed that Johnny and Dekeon had left.

Jerry told me that Johnny worried that our automatic Dog washing service would put him out of business. I hoped he was just kidding because I thought Johnny was a neat guy and I only wanted good things for him.

Dekeon and I ran together for seven years. Then one day we saw Johnny, and it was the only time we'd seen him without his great smile and without Dekeon. He informed us that Dekeon had succumbed to cancer. I felt sad like when I couldn't see Rita anymore. Besides Jerry, Dekeon was my best friend, and I was about to experience some difficult mourning. I suddenly understood what families undergo when they lose their loved ones.

CHAPTER 17

Coyote at Hawks Head

When I hear someone say "He's only a Dog,"
I know that they just don't know Dogs
and they especially don't know me.

—Shiloh

One of my favorite pastimes involves accompanying Jerry and his friends as they golf at Hawks Head, an Arthur Hills course that is ten minutes away from the lake house.

All summer long we spend every Tuesday and Thursday morning on this great course. Our usual fivesome includes Jerry, Larry, Terry, Win, and me. They joke about replacing Win with someone named Harry, Barry, or Kerry, so that they can call themselves the Rhyming Quartet.

If a golfer hits his ball into the heather or the woods, they send me to retrieve it. I always come back with a ball, and sometimes it's actually the one they lost.

As the golfers leave the fifth green, I'm ready to take off, as this is the spot where I run around. Before Jerry releases me he always asks the others, "Anyone want to wager with five to one odds that Shiloh won't turn right at the end of the cart path?"

Since I almost always go right, Jerry only lost this bet once, when I chased after a huge black squirrel on the left.

On one particular day I ran down the long cart path toward the sixth tee. There were large woods on my right and I veered off the path and into the trees. Then I walked over the hill that obscures the location of the tee, where I met the golfers, who were preparing to tee off.

After a great ride and a couple of runs, we finished and returned our cart. The young pro, Jason, asked the guys, "Did anyone see a coyote on the course today?"

They answered, "No way. They're nocturnal." They all agreed that they had never seen one on the course at any time.

Jason continued, "The foursome playing right behind you were from Chicago. They swore they saw a coyote run out of the woods near the fifth green and go over the hill toward the sixth tee."

I smiled to myself, and thought, "Well, City Slickers, you've now seen Shiloh, the Hawk's Head Coyote."

When we go north and stay at the hunting camp, I have to put up with my master poorly imitating a coyote. I will be sound asleep when all of a sudden I hear this blood-curdling scream. The worst part is that when he does this, Jerry is certain that he hears a pack of coyotes answering him. As the look-alike coyote of Hawk's Head, I find this embarrassing.

CHAPTER 18
Jillian and Her Dogs

In hospitals all across the country,
something exciting is happening.
Therapy Dogs and patients are connecting
in ways that enhance human healing.

—Jillian

Early on in my therapy career, I met a woman named Jillian at Holland Hospital. She was in charge of a Special Pet Therapy Program.

An observer for Therapy Dogs, Inc. of Cheyenne, Wyoming, one of the major therapy Dog certifiers in the country, had recently certified me. I was qualified and ready to do my thing for the hospital. Young, spunky, and full of attitude, I felt that I could do everything my way, but I was way wrong. Jillian had a very structured program, which included me visiting three times as a sort of intern before I was ready to be on my own.

In addition to scheduling my one-hour visits, Jillian came along to observe me. We always went to Jillian's office before we started our assignment and again after the visit so that we could review my work.

After we had volunteered for several visits, Jillian announced, "Shiloh, I've heard such good reports from everyone about your work. I'm giving you your own special red bandana, which reads, 'Holland Hospital Healing Environment.'

I wasn't sure what that meant, but when she gave me a Dog biscuit before my assignment and shook my paw, I knew that it was a good sign. Blond and very pretty, Jillian always smelled like apple pie and ice cream. Biscuits always seemed to sharpen my views about women and how good they smell.

Jillian gave us the list of post-op patients who had requested a visit from a four-legged doctor, and while she came along on our visits, she stayed mostly in the background. I think I looked very handsome with my new red bandana around my neck.

One day when we arrived at her office, Jillian said, "Shiloh, you've received your diploma," and she presented Jerry and me my own personalized calling cards. She read it aloud:

> *"From your four-legged Doctor. I enjoyed our visit!*
> *I hope I helped brighten your day too.*
> *Woof and cheers.*
> *Shiloh, DOG."*

I learned that Jillian's dad was a retired veterinarian, and she grew up with lots of Dogs. She loved her Dogs and I loved her.

CHAPTER 19

The Soup Lady

*The Dog wags his tail, not for you,
but for your bread (crackers).*

—Portuguese Proverb

erry had been retired for several years, but he loved going back to the restaurants that he helped open. One time when we were at one of the restaurants in Kalamazoo, Jerry sat in the booth closest to the front door and I followed my usual routine, responding obediently to his command that I sit at the end of the booth. His next command was, "Shiloh, under the table."

I was half-asleep, wondering about the elderly lady in the booth next to us. While I was sitting there, before going under the table, I heard her talking to me. "What a nice Dog," she said.

The pretty hostess (I've never seen an ugly one) came to our table and informed Jerry that he had a call on the restaurant phone up front by the cashier.

Suddenly, after Jerry left, this sweet elderly lady dropped down onto the floor on all fours and put soup crackers right in front of my nose, which I graciously accepted. She told me what a good-looking Dog I was, and I agreed with her completely as I gobbled up the crackers. Then I heard a waitress say, "Ma'am, can I help you?"

Remaining on her knees, the elderly lady turned her head up and responded, "I need more soup crackers, and by the way my soup's cold." Around this time, my master returned to the table. He seemed uncomfortable at the sight of this lady's rear end protruding from his booth. He said, "Ma'am, can I help you?"

"Yes," she responded, "I need more soup crackers."

At that moment, the waitress returned with a hot bowl of soup and more crackers.

As Jerry helped the soup lady to her feet, she seemed embarrassed and apologized immediately. "I'm sorry, I just loved the look of your Dog and I got carried away."

I wanted to inform her that I have this effect on people, but of course I couldn't communicate this to her.

She told Jerry, "I'm ninety-one years old and my retirement home doesn't allow Dogs. So since I love them so much, I never pass up an opportunity to talk to them."

Jerry sounded sympathetic and reassured her that she had done nothing wrong. My master began telling her that I was a Therapy Dog who visited hospices and hospitals to give comfort to some very sick people.

"I knew he was something special. I could tell by the way he held his head," she said. Of course, upon hearing that, I felt good and tried to smile at her, but she wasn't looking at me.

She finished her soup as Jerry's order was arriving. She began gathering up her belongings and I noticed that she put the remaining crackers in her pocket. As she passed by our table, she hesitated and apologized to Jerry again, holding his attention while secretly pulling the soup crackers from her pocket and flipping them gracefully under the table to me. I was the only one who saw this. At ninety-one, she had pretty good aim.

I finished up the crackers as quietly as I could while Jerry ate his lunch and read the local paper.

CHAPTER 20
Barnes and Noble

Dogs are not our whole life
but they make our lives whole.

—Roger Caras

I always went into Barnes and Noble with Jerry. He and Barb are both big readers. On one occasion, when we entered the store, this woman who looked like a grandmother stroked me on the head and said, "Shiloh, you'd be perfect as the warm-up act for my weekly pre-school reading group."

I accepted her offer, since I thought she looked like a perfect grandmother, with her gray hair, glasses, and warm, trusting smile. She was also good at petting. I then faced the dilemma of having to figure out how to I convey this situation to my master, who had his nose stuck in a book called, *How to Make a Living as a Blackjack Player.* I was aware that he knew enough about this subject to write his own book, which he would probably title, *How to Go Broke While Trying to Make a Living Playing Blackjack.*

When he went up to pay for his purchases, the nice grandmother turned out to be our cashier. Her name was Gayle and she conveniently solved my communication problem by letting Jerry know about her idea. "I've talked to Shiloh and he likes the idea," she said with a wonderful smile. I assumed that she could read minds. I made a mental note that I would have to control my thoughts when I was around Gayle. Sure enough, the following week I was her warm-up act for eight cute kids between the ages of two and five. I carried a stuffed animal around the children's book area and let all the kids pet and hug me.

Gayle was clairvoyant as she announced, "I knew Shiloh would like all of you and he does." I thought to myself, "Wow, she can read my mind!"

By the time Gayle started reading a book about Dogs (how appropriate), I was sound asleep, dreaming that the weight of the world was upon my shoulders. When Gayle said, "We're done, Shiloh, time to wake up," I realized that six of the eight children were laying on me. When they climbed off of my back, the weight of my young world magically disappeared. I continued to be Gayle's warm-up act for quite a while after that, and there was never a dull moment around her and those kids.

One day I was invited to be a listener Dog at the Fennville District Library. One of the innovative programs that was available at the library featured Therapy Dogs and their handlers. It's called *Paws and Read: Kids Plus Dogs = Paw-rrific Reading Adventures.*

That afternoon, Ms. Kooyers explained that after school, the fourth and fifth graders would pick out a story to read to me. It was a kind of reward for all of my volunteer therapy work, and it helped the kids display their reading skills.

The last reader, John, asked my permission to read from the Bible, and my master quickly said, "With a biblical name like Shiloh, it would be very appropriate."

John was mature beyond his ten years, and he read Psalm 23 with such passion that I detected tears in the eyes of my master and the librarian. John thanked us for the opportunity to read and we wanted to thank him in return, but he left too quickly. Ms. Kooyers told us that John's mother had passed away without warning only two weeks earlier and this had been his first day back in school.

CHAPTER 21

David and Goliath

You think Dogs will not be in Heaven?
I tell you, they will be there long before any of us.

—Robert Louis Stevenson

J erry went fishing in Canada with a bunch of his friends, including his minister, David. One night in camp, after a successful day of fishing and a great dinner, several of the guys were sitting around a blazing campfire telling stories.

Someone asked, "David is there such a thing as reincarnation?"

David, a minister who was a bit of a politician, turned the question around by saying, "Let's assume there is such a possibility as being reincarnated. Let's go around the circle and find out who everyone would want to come back as."

There were some interesting answers, including the President of the United States, a professional golfer, a

Hollywood star, and a woman. Then it was Jerry's turn. Without any hesitation he simply said, "Jerry Hill's Dog."

When I heard this at a later time, I thought that it was a moving and empathetic answer. It warmed my heart to hear that my master wanted to know me so intimately that he would like to actually be me.

David was a regular tennis player in Jerry's group. He was an excellent player and also had the benefit of being young. His wife invited the entire tennis group to the surprise fortieth birthday party she was planning for David. She and their three children surprised David with a Bouvier Dog named Goliath. Goliath and I became regular ball Dogs on Jerry's tennis court, and sometimes we were even more entertaining than the tennis matches.

David had a Bouvier when he was growing up, so he grew very close to this puppy. He began including Goliath in occasional church services, and he even built some sermons around him. He was a big hit with all the parishioners and his presence added a new flavor to the old biblical story of David and Goliath.

There were many sayings that David used to illustrate how Dogs are part of religion, including:

"Dogs are miracles with paws," "Man is a Dog's idea of what God should be," and "The Dog is the only animal that has seen his God."

And David, being a philosopher as well as a minister, had several other favorite quotations;

"Wherever you go, go with all your heart" (Confucius)

"What we have to learn to do, we learn by doing" (Aristotle)

"A loving atmosphere in your home creates a strong foundation for your life" (David)

CHAPTER 22

Bankruptcy

The more one gets to know of men and what they do,
the more one values Dogs.

—Alphonse Toussenel

J erry had been retired for ten years in 2002 when he began to spend some time back at his old business. The company began experiencing financial problems and they asked Jerry if he would return to the Board of Directors, as he had helped run the company the majority of his thirty-three-year career. He agreed to return as an advisory board member.

There were many meetings, and on the cooler days I got to ride from the lake house to Battle Creek, though I always had to stay in the car. I observed that Jerry was very serious on these trips, especially on the drive back home. He would talk aloud, presumably to me, as I was the only other one in the car. I hadn't a clue what he was talking about, but he always said, "Shy, thanks for listening."

Around this same time, Jerry also attended Olivet College board of trustees meetings. Olivet was a small college with a beautiful campus in the middle of the Michigan farmlands. It was unique in that its entire curriculum was based on a book called *Education for Individual and Social Responsibility*.

I had been with him at these meetings since I was a puppy. We always arrived on Fridays between 8:30 and 9:00 a.m. for coffee and goodies before the meeting. Everyone tried to give me a snack, but my master was vigilant and he intervened. I would think to myself, "Drat!"

Chairman David would call the meeting to order, and I would lie under my master's table. All of the tables had white tablecloths hanging to the floor, and they were arranged in a large closed rectangle. I would position myself with either my nose or my tail protruding from the tablecloth into the enclosed area. The chairman would instruct them to introduce themselves, and he always included me. I liked that. As the years went by, he would make note of my most recent accomplishments, and everyone would go "ooh" and "ah" and applaud me. Within minutes I would be fast asleep with my special college dream of coeds fussing over me and calling me "girl magnet," one of my many aliases. I would occasionally evoke laughter by moaning and groaning when I was having a puppy dream.

After serving for eight years, Jerry retired from the college board and was honored as a Trustee Emeritus, at which point we began to attend only one or two meetings per year. After a few years, Chairman David pointed out that I had been coming to the meetings for longer than 80 percent of the board members. I had hoped that he would refer to me as an honorary board member, but apparently something called a by-law didn't provide such honors for Dogs.

On my last trip with Jerry to the restaurant's board meeting, I sensed that these gatherings were much more intense than the Olivet College trustee meetings, and they were getting worse all the time. Although I was never invited to attend, I got the general drift of the situation and it was not good. Many changes had been made. Jerry provided his counsel and did his best to turn things around, but the company was heading toward bankruptcy. Jerry made many conference calls from home, and Barb always asked, "What's happening and what does this mean?" She was concerned because most of their income depended on the success of the restaurants.

After a conference call would end, Jerry would become downbeat and troubled instead of being upbeat like he normally was. He would respond to Barb, "Bad things and trouble for all," referring to the employees, the customers, and ultimately the stockholders of the company. And then it happened. The company filed for bankruptcy. My life would be changed forever.

Chapter 23

Damn the Torpedoes

No one appreciates the very special genius
of your conversation as the Dog does.

—Christopher Morley

The next few days were very different. We had our normal routine, but my master was pensive and subdued. I decided that he was simply like this when he was deep in thought. He spent a lot of time writing numbers on a legal pad and then wadding them up and throwing them toward a paper basket, which he missed more than he hit. Even this lack of accuracy perturbed him.

Every day we would go outside and walk around the 300 feet of property that Barb and Jerry owned on Lake Michigan. Their 1,500-square-foot converted cottage was situated smack in the middle of this land.

Before his retirement, Jerry was a workaholic and his office was only five minutes from the home in Battle Creek.

He usually worked five full days a week, including two dinner hours in the various restaurant cities. Three ten-hour workdays and two twelve-hour workdays added up to over fifty hours of work per week. In addition, he usually went to his office on Saturday and Sunday. Barb was determined to get him to cut back on his hours, but Jerry's work philosophy was a carryover from his college days, when he always had two or three part-time jobs. He traveled between all of the restaurants, which would eventually include over sixty locations. He felt that he should communicate with every member of management, which included more than 285 people. There were more than four thousand employees and he felt a personal responsibility for all of them.

"Barb, I'll retire early and then we'll have all the time in the world," he would say.

Barb had a plan. She wanted to find a place on the water so that he could spend more time staying at home and less time working. Her philosophy was, "Find the lake house and he will come."

She did find it. It was rundown and it had not been winterized, but it sat in the middle of three hundred feet of property on beautiful Lake Michigan, and it was only an hour's drive from Battle Creek. Jerry liked the property and he made an offer. The realtor was very young and this seemed to be one of his first listings. He informed Jerry that although his offer was "in the ball park" for the cottage, the land, including three hundred feet of waterfront property, was held in trust and the trustee wanted to sell the cottage and the two lots north and south of the house as one parcel. Jerry told Barb the bad news.

She said, "Let's buy the whole three hundred feet!"

"What would we do with two worthless lots on Lake Michigan?" he responded.

"Sell them after we buy the whole parcel of land?" Barb responded.

Jerry offered an extra ten thousand dollars for the two worthless lots on Lake Michigan. The young realtor said, "Your offer is way too low and I won't even bother the trustee with it."

Jerry replied, "The water in Lake Michigan is very high now and the trend is going even higher. You'll be stuck with these lots. Furthermore, legally and ethically, you must show the offer I have made."

A month later, the realtor called and said, "If you sweeten your offer a bit, I think you might be successful."

Jerry reminded the realtor of the recent rains and the water that was rising. "I couldn't possibly go a penny higher," Jerry responded.

Two days later, Jerry's offer was accepted.

Barb and Jerry winterized the house and built another bedroom, a porch and a great deck overlooking the big lake. They kept the two other lots. Barb was smart and her plan had worked.

Until he retired in 1992, Jerry commuted for six months out of the year from the lake cottage to Battle Creek, and in 1999, they changed their principal residence and spent the majority of their time at the Lake, while still keeping the Battle Creek house, where they had raised their three boys.

After many weeks of seeing Jerry in an anxious state, I finally saw a large smile on his face. He said to Barb, "Do you know what the famous Admiral David Farragut said when confronted with enemy firing torpedoes at his fleet during the Civil War?"

"No," Barb said, "but he was obviously in the navy and you're going to tell me his plan."

"Yep. That plan was to say 'damn the torpedoes. Full speed ahead.' And that's what we are going to do. First, we've lost all of our retirement income and benefits through the damage caused by the bankruptcy. We need to replace that income as best we can and reduce our expenditures."

"Second, we'll sell the cottage and north lot, which includes two hundred feet of property on Lake Michigan. It's now worth big money compared to thirty years ago. We'll build our dream house on the southern lot with a quarter of the proceeds and use the remaining three-fourths of the money to help replace our lost retirement income. Last, we'll sell our Battle Creek home after our dream house is completed." Jerry took a deep breath and seemed vastly relieved at having laid out his plans for Barb.

Barb was amazed. She laughed with great relief. Jerry was happy and upbeat and so was I. Good times were coming again.

Damn the torpedoes. Full speed ahead.

CHAPTER 24

Kate Paint

The Dog was created specifically for children.
He is the God of frolic.

—Henry Ward Beecher

While building their dream house at Lake Michigan, Barb told her three granddaughters that they could decorate their own bedroom upstairs. Their furniture consisted of three twin beds from the old cottage and a crib. Barb and Jerry told the girls that they could do whatever they wanted with their room.

Carly, Lindsay, and Kate were twelve, ten and six years of age. At four and two years old, the grandsons were not into the idea of decorating yet.

The new lake house was only a month old and the two oldest girls brought two friends over to help them decorate their room. On the Saturday of their week of vacation, they planned and painted their bedroom.

Char and Tim dropped by. They asked if we would take care of Kate and said that they would return in a few hours. Kate was a lot of fun and she had very high energy. After a while Barb and Jerry looked around and asked each other, "Where's Kate?" There was a sudden feeling of desperation because Jerry had thought that Kate was with Barb, and Barb had thought that Kate was with Jerry. I too had lost track of her. We were all concerned that a six-year-old near the lake could be a recipe for disaster. Jerry ran down to the beach and Barb searched the basement and outside and they even asked me, "Where's Kate?"

For some reason, I headed upstairs toward the older kids in their new room. Jerry followed and said, "Good idea, Shy. We'll form a posse with the kids and search in the woods."

As we got close to the room, we heard Lindsay say, "Now Kate, paint inside these lines." Jerry was tremendously relieved. He quietly looked in on his granddaughter with Down syndrome being helped by her older cousins as they helped her paint a scene on the wall. As he peered around the corner, Kate spied Jerry and said, "Look Pa, me paint, Kate paint." I'll never forget what she said, nor will Jerry. She was so happy there, painting with her cousins. Jerry waved and stepped back into the hallway. Tears were running down his cheeks. I gave my master a lick on the hand to show him my compassion.

Jerry met Barb on the way downstairs. He simply gave her the thumbs up and pointed toward the kid's bedroom.

I went back upstairs with Barb. They had painted a scene at the beach with caricatures of the five grandchildren on one wall, and they had painted the opposite wall completely blue. They told Barb that the blue wall would provide the background for the next mural, which they would have to wait until the following summer visit to paint. A few days after they headed home, Barb asked Jerry to help her make up the beds with fresh linens. Of course I went along. I don't know why, but I never felt comfortable upstairs when I was by myself.

Jerry pulled the twin bed away from the blue wall, and he and Barb convulsed into laughter. The girls had painted on only the visible part of the wall and not behind the bed.

I was more concerned about the wall that contained a caricature of me, which I discovered to be unflattering. I found out later that their friend Taylor had painted me. I know that my good buddy Kate would have done a better job. The next time she came to the lake house I was going to attempt to say to her, "I want you to redo my picture, Kate. Kate paint!"

CHAPTER 25

The Big Fall

I'm so sorry.

—Shiloh

The summer of 2003 was our first summer in the lake house. The decorating clan of grandchildren had left for their separate homes and Barb was planning her first dinner party.

She had a reasonably strict rule that she referred to as 'six at six,' which meant that a maximum of six people, not including me, were allowed at the dinner party, and everyone arrived at 6:00 p.m. However, for the first dinner party in the new lake house, she invited three of the neighbor couples, which brought the number of people present to nine, including me.

The great room had a huge table that could seat up to a baker's dozen, or twelve people, with me situated in my usual spot under the table.

Barb had worked hard on her special recipes for two days before the party. She is a great cook and Jerry even refers to her as a gourmet chef. Sometimes he teases her by saying that she should open her own gourmet restaurant. She looks at him in a special way that only a wife can look at her husband, which I interpret as her saying, "You must be absolutely downright crazy! Remember we've been down that restaurant road before."

When the guests arrived, the evening began with cocktails and hors oeuvres, followed by salad, the entre, and Barb's unbelievable chocolate bread pudding for dessert.

As I mentioned earlier, I remained under the table and out of the way. But this was cocktail hour when people were telling stories, and I wanted to be close to the action.

With drink in hand, Barb walked from the great room toward the kitchen to check on the food in the oven. The floors in the great room were medium brown, exactly the color of my fur. At that moment, I wished that I had been born a completely black or white Dog. Barb, gregarious as ever and chatting while she headed for the kitchen tripped over me and fell heavily to the floor. In unison everyone said, "Barb, are you all right?" Like the great trooper that she is, she said, "Yes."

Jerry helped her up and settled her into the dining room chair at the end of the table. I watched her face very closely and saw that she was in a lot of pain. Barb's philosophy was that the party must go on. Jerry is a great cook in his own right, so he took over, putting the finishing touches on the meal and serving all of the courses. By dessert time it was evident to everyone that the fall had done some damage.

Barb kept saying that she was all right and that once she got into bed everything would be fine.

The dinner party broke up early. Expressing their concern for Barb, everyone left into the early summer evening and missed the Lake Michigan sunset.

After everyone was gone, Barb couldn't hold back her feelings of extreme pain and discomfort any longer. Jerry suggested they go to the emergency room, but she resisted, so he helped her to bed.

I could see that she was in a bad state, but she insisted that she would be fine by morning. She was still fully dressed as she slipped under the covers with my master's help and nicely ordered him to leave her alone. I'm convinced that she didn't want him to see and hear her pain. Barb had always been a person who never complained. However, I never left the side of the bed and she seemed to be happy with my presence, even though I was responsible for her big fall. Never did she complain either then or since about my part in the 'life changing' event.

She never fell asleep, and when Jerry checked on her for the twentieth time against her orders, she sobbed, "Honey, I've got to go to the hospital."

He called for an ambulance because her pain was getting more intense and it seemed unwise to move her without professional assistance. The first responders, led by our friend, Benito, were there in a flash, even though it was close to midnight. They carefully loaded my ailing mistress onto a gurney and into the waiting ambulance.

"Sorry Shy," Jerry said, "We might be awhile, so you're in charge here at the house."

I jumped onto Jerry's bed and attempted to sleep but to no avail. The look of pain on Barb's face and the great concern on Jerry's face worried me terribly. As I grew older, I had become more in tune with my ability to read humans faces, and I found that if they looked into my eyes I could read their emotions deeply and clearly. At that moment, I wished that I didn't have that talent.

Eventually, I think I did finally slip into sleep. Much later, I heard Jerry talk about how when they arrived at the ER at Holland Hospital, Barb was admitted to one of the rooms to be tested and x-rayed and await the doctor's diagnosis. Having volunteered at that hospital, I knew how great the staff and facilities were. Barb was in the best possible hands.

Soon the results were in and they showed a crack in the greater Tricanter on the side of her hip. It would probably require surgery. Meanwhile, since Barb is a heart patient and was still in considerable pain, she was transferred upstairs to a room where they gave her pain medication and further tests.

Before coming home early in the afternoon the next day, Jerry called Alice, my favorite next-door neighbor, to ask her to feed and walk me in the morning.

Barb's face was still filled with pain and anguish, and I carefully approached her with my tail wagging. She forced a smile and said, "Shy, I'm going to my bed and I want you nearby."

Usually I was Jerry's constant companion, but during the immediate period when Barb returned from the hospital, I stayed by her side. Because she unconditionally accepted me in spite of what I had inadvertently done to her, I loved her more than ever.

I watched Jerry and Barb very closely. I believe I love them more than they love themselves.

CHAPTER 26
Hospital and Surgery

*The storms of our life proves
the strength of our anchor.*

—Unknown

The surgeon was confident that a forty-five-minute operation could repair Barb's greater Tricanter in her hip. She went into surgery around 3:00 p.m. on a Friday. I was allowed to stay in the waiting room with Jerry since I visited this area on a regular basis for my therapy work. At 6:00 p.m. they closed this area for the evening, and we moved to a smaller room all by ourselves.

Apparently Barb was the only person still in surgery. There were many updates in person and then by telephone and then nothing but waiting for a long time. I could see in his eyes that my master was understandably worried.

On the day of the fateful fall, the dinner guests had complimented me on how much my therapy visits meant to people and they declared that I was a hero. I felt that I was far from being a hero. Watching Jerry closely, I felt very scared.

People without Dogs don't realize how deep into each other's eyes a Dog and master can see and communicate their feelings. Normally, this is a wonderful thing, but in times of pain it can be very scary.

"Shiloh, let's cut out the stare down," Jerry said. "I know you mean well, but it's bugging me."

I lowered my eyes and softly set my nose in his lap. I sat there for a long time while Jerry gently patted my head. When people pet me, it is good therapy for both of us. I was feeling better and I hoped that Jerry was too.

Finally, around 7:00 p.m. the primary surgeon told us that there had been some complications. Barb's bones were too soft to hold the screws and claws were required to hold everything together. Two surgeons ended up doing the best they could and they felt the result had a good chance of working.

Unfortunately, a year later Barb's hip deteriorated and then broke and she had to go through a long siege of discomfort, followed by an orthopedic revisionist surgeon performing a total hip replacement. The surgeon, Jeffery, was a miracle worker with his expertise and bedside manner. Although his work had been outstanding, considerable challenges awaited Barb in her process of rehabilitation, which included two stints at Freedom Village (as I talk about in chapter 44).

Because this was a most difficult period in Barb's life she prefers not to talk about it. So, instead, I'll tell you about her recovery period in Florida and how it turned a tough time period into a positive result.

CHAPTER 27

Mayor Nancy's Rules

Properly trained, a man can be Dog's best friend.

—Corey Ford

O ne of Jerry's good friends, John, invited Jerry and Barb down to Stuart, Florida, so that Barb could spend some of her recovery period there. Because he had spent a lot of time in Florida opening up new restaurants, Jerry wasn't crazy about Florida, but he accepted John's invitation because he thought that it would be great for Barb.

As soon as we arrived, my master took me for a walk so that I could do my business. We walked in through an open gate and explored the swimming pool. Although I was not on a leash, Jerry was commanding me to heel. A woman approached us and said, "Are you a new owner?"

"No," Jerry said, "we are renting from a friend for a month."

"Renters cannot have Dogs here. Only owners can," she informed us rather curtly.

At that moment, Jerry said, "Sit Shiloh, shake Shiloh." I dutifully obeyed, and although we both thought she had taken the bait, she smiled and said, "Sorry, no Dogs for renters."

I learned later that the woman's name was Nancy and that many folks referred to her as the Mayor of Lakeside, the name of the condo complex association. Jerry told her a couple of harmless fibs. He told her that John was his brother-in-law, and that I was a registered therapy Dog who was cross-trained as a service animal. All that information seemed to confuse Nancy.

Her response was, "Keep him on a leash and make sure he's wearing his therapy jacket at all times. He can't come into the pool area." She added that she wouldn't complain about me, but she couldn't guarantee that the other owners would not report me.

Many years later, Nancy and her husband Bill became good friends with Barb and Jerry.

Jerry made all this possible. I have learned much from my master. Barb always accuses Jerry of exaggerating, but she still thinks he's a great guy. And so do I.

That first night in Florida, Jerry, Barb, and I went out to dinner with John and his partner Barbara. Everyone instantly bonded with each other. John had lost his wife two years earlier and had then met Barbara, and he invited us to their wedding party the next week. By the end of the month, I had a whole circle of friends in Florida, and I planned to educate them all about what a therapy Dog does.

We were extra careful for the entire month at the condo and I became very popular, turning on the charm and validating Jerry's pet name for me: con man.

By the end of January, with Barb's recovery being ahead of schedule, they decided that they would like to buy a condo in Stuart. After we returned to Michigan, their friends, John and Barbara, began looking for a place for them to buy.

In April, John called to say he had found them the perfect place. It was in Tennis Villas, which was nearby and similar to the condos in Lakeside. Impulsively, Jerry bought it within days and I was concerned that since it was only 990 square feet there might not be enough room for me. I always sleep on my master's bed, and I hoped that it wouldn't be too high here to jump up on. When I'm tired I lay down at the foot of Jerry's bed. He's a night owl and stays up late. Before he gets into bed, he spreads a large beach towel on the end of his bed. I pretend to pay no attention to him and I think I'm very clever. Once Jerry's asleep I jump carefully up onto the beach towel and sleep there all night. Before he wakes up, I quietly climb down and resume my innocent position on the floor. I've heard Jerry tell people this habit of mine on numerous occasions, so I know that he endorses it, but we continue to play the game anyway. After Jerry rises in the morning, I climb up into the place where he slept the night. I love to lie on his pillow. Again, I have to give him credit for knowing more about me than I know about myself. I've heard him tell friends about how once he turns on the water for the shower, he slides the door open and gazes on his wonderful Dog. Of course, by this time, I am fast asleep on my master's pillow.

CHAPTER 28

Bear Attack!

Turn the other cheek.

—Shiloh

A t the lake house in Michigan, the nights were still perfect for a fire in the big stone fireplace. But first, let me tell you about how we got to this point.

Jerry and I used to wander the south lot pondering and planning the eventual construction of the lake house. He wanted to build a fireplace and he knew where it should be. However, there was a large, beautiful ash tree at that exact spot. He knew that it would have to be cut down, and on these walks he would talk out loud, apparently preparing the tree for its ultimate demise. I felt like this was very weird but out of respect for the soon-to-be-harvested tree, I never peed on it.

When the final plans were completed for the house, my master made a deal with the man he hired to clear the land.

(Jerry had lots of nicknames for me, but little did he know I also had many aliases for him. In this case, I called him the Dealmaker.)

I heard Jerry make this proposal: "That's a beautiful and valuable ash tree...so...after you drop it, you can haul it to your friend's sawmill. Make me a mantle for my fireplace-to-be and you guys can keep the rest of the good saw logs. Make a pile of the remaining not-so-good felled trees and I'll cut and split them for firewood. Even deal, no labor expense." Two yeps later, they shook hands and the beautiful ash tree would always be close to its birthplace.

Jerry loved to split wood. With an axe in his hands, I think he saw himself as a lumberjack of old.

We set up shop near the two-track road away from the house. Jerry had a large wooden block surrounded with wood waiting to be split for firewood. I was always moved far enough away from the splitting area that no flying chips could harm me. Little did I realize that harm would come from an entirely different source.

A neighbor had a Dog named Bear who was almost my age. Bear and I had been good buddies for a few years however, when the woman of the house became a widow, Bear started to become very protective of her and he began to growl at me. I was careful not to provoke him and I learned to keep my distance.

On one particular day, Bear appeared out of nowhere and Jerry hollered, "Shiloh, stay." I obeyed my master and then I heard Bear's owner calling, "Bear," but instead of going to her he ran toward me. A barking Dog with his head held high is never a threat, but Bear held his head down and he was growling.

Before I could get up from the ground, he had my face in his mouth. I could feel his teeth puncturing my flesh. The pain was sharp, shooting up into my head. I was stunned for a moment before I noticed that Jerry was kicking Bear with his shoes and yelling, "Bear, no!" By the time Bear's owner was nearby and Jerry had separated us, I was bleeding profusely from my mouth and cheek. I had never bled before. I had no clue why Bear had done this, and I did not know what would come next.

I was quickly loaded into the car and we drove off to the vet's office. I became anxious. Although I like all of my vets, I don't like the things they do to me. The thought of vaccinations and rectal thermometers brings up bad memories. What happened next was an entirely new experience for me and it was horrible. I had to get stitches, and lots of them!

Feeling guilty, Jerry told the vet that he had never kicked or struck a Dog before. The vet assured him that he had no other choice.

I left the office feeling numb and woozy, and I fell asleep as soon as Jerry helped me into the car. I dreamt that I was on the Serengeti Plains in East Africa, fending off a pride of lions that were trying to take down one of my wildebeest buddies.

I awakened when Jerry carried me into the house. Very thirsty, I headed for my water bowl, but making my mouth move to lap up water was very difficult. The liquid kept dripping out of the side of my mouth.

In time I got better, and due to my biblical name, I considered turning the other cheek when I next saw Bear. However, since I didn't want to have my other cheek bitten, I avoided him at all costs.

Jerry was sensitive to Bear's mistress, and he never shared with her the details about the extent of my injuries. She had recently lost her husband and Jerry felt that she didn't need this extra concern in her life.

Bear eventually passed away and his owner got another Dog, a gentle, fun-loving, and playful guy. I never shared with him the story about his predecessor.

CHAPTER 29

Nosy

If a Dog smells another Dog on you,
they don't get mad; they just think it's interesting.

—Why Some Men Have Dogs and Not Wives

My universe is full of smells: good ones, bad ones, and different ones that I haven't yet categorized. My sense of smell is my number-one method of investigation. I'm continually sniffing everything and everybody. Just smelling my master's clothing causes my tail to start wagging.

However, there is a downside to my great sense of smell. Over the years, Jerry has kept a diary of the terminally ill people I have rejected. *Rejection* is his word, not mine. I accept everyone unconditionally. Let me explain.

At one Hospice facility in Florida, we received our list of people who had requested a hospet visit. I'll never forget the experience I had with one dying man on this particular day. He was the fourth person we saw that day, and he was in room number four. Jerry always knocks lightly on the door of each room to make sure that the patient wants to be visited by a hospet. The family who were assembled in the patient's room answered that they did want a visit, and I bounded in, wagging my tail, shaking my paws, and receiving lots of hugs and pets. Jerry called me over to the life-threatened patient's bed. I eagerly ran over, and when the man touched my head, a sharp signal went straight to my brain. My super-sniffer sense told me that something was very wrong with this patient, and I instantly backed away. Jerry was embarrassed, as he didn't understand my behavior, and was obliged to make a flimsy excuse, which the family accepted.

When we returned for our next hospet visit a few days later, Jerry inquired as to the status of the patient in room number four.

"He died within an hour after your last visit," the nurse informed us.

The same scenario played out in the exact same manner about a month later, and Jerry discussed this with my Florida veterinarian. His educated guess was that I could smell the impending death that was caused by cancer, and the odor was repugnant.

This seemed to be a great dichotomy. Here I was, unconditionally accepting of everyone and on my way to becoming the busiest hospet Dog of all time, and I was actually backing away from some patients because of my super-sniffer sense.

I heard the vet say, "Animals react in different ways to impending death. Some reject it and some embrace it."

Over the years some staff members have asked Jerry to share information with them about these specific occurrences, as it might help them in their work. My record has been 100 percent accurate. Every person I have backed away from has died within twenty-four hours.

I don't feel guilty about backing away from some life-threatened patients. I think that only humans suffer from guilt. When I smell an overpowering odor, I simply react to it. I can no more stop this behavior than I can stop eating. It is an instinct, but some patients have a less powerful odor and I am able to accept their pats and hugs.

My master tells me that my reactions provide a special service to the hospice staff. Sometimes special abilities tell us more than we want to know, but as long as we use these talents for the good of mankind, it's okay to be nosy.

CHAPTER 30

Business at Alice's

The amount of time it takes for a Dog to
do his business is directly proportional to the outside tempera-
ture
and the suitability of the owners outerwear.

—Betsy Canas Garmon

When Barb and Jerry built their new lake house
on the south lot, they cut off the view to the
north somewhat from their southern neighbors,
Alice and Dick, who had owned their home for over forty
years. Jerry, the building planner, was sensitive to their
concerns.

One day Alice asked Jerry if he would consider putting
his outdoor air conditioner unit on the north side of the
new house so that the fan noise wouldn't bother them.

Jerry, always the consummate politician, told Alice
that he would give her request much consideration. He had

already decided that he would put it on the north side, but he liked to make points when he could. The next day he visited Alice and gave her the good news that he would comply with her request. Alice was happy and so was I when she gave me one of Jingle's Dog biscuits. Her Dog Jingle was a small Dog. He loved to bark at me, but he never meant any harm.

After we moved into the new house, I plotted out my morning walks. Once breakfast was over, Jerry let me out on my own. I hopped through the split-rail fence and headed toward Alice's flower garden. After irrigating much of the garden, I moved toward the weeds just past the house and did my business there. Meanwhile, Jingle was returning the favor on our lawn. In all these years, I have never heard Alice or Jerry complain about where we did our business.

Along with their daughters, Alice and Dick had lots of Dogs: Sweetie, Kiwi, Sydney, Linus (who is sixteen years old and still going) and Chester. Chester was a Tibetan terrier whom Betsy, one of their daughters, was training to become a Therapy Dog. I hoped I was her inspiration.

Named for the breeder, another unusual Dog was called a Jennifer Dog. Alice's family had one of these designer Dogs over as a visitor for Thanksgiving. I looked him over closely and wasn't sure that he was real. He had been purchased for $1,500 and was aptly named Bentley. He was not only unique but also expensive.

Tammy, the other daughter, trained Dogs for a group called Paws for Cause. She had little success with graduating her Dogs so that they could work with clients. It sounds like tough love and tough work to me. The Dogs that flunked out became part of Tammy's Dog family. Actually, Luna, a

Labrador retriever who is probably a distant relative of mine on my dad's side of the family, became a very successful Agility Dog. An Agility Dog is one that is trained on an obstacle course for competition. Tammy was elated when she saw Luna again for the first time since Luna had left her nest two years ago. Luna expressed her recognition of Tammy by wagging her tail and whimpering.

One of Tammy's Dogs that flunked, an apricot-colored standard poodle named Milo, was a real piece of work. He could run like the wind. He could run from the lake house to the beach in about 3.4 seconds. I sometimes followed him at my fastest time, which was about thirty-four seconds. We would run free until one of our masters shouted: "Milo— Shiloh, Come!"

I loved to go everywhere with Jerry and Barb, but occasionally they would go on a day trip or an overnight trip to Chicago and leave me at home to jump onto Jerry's bed and get caught up on some extra rest. On these occasions, Alice would take care of feeding me and taking me on walks. As soon as I would hear the south deck door being unlocked, I knew that it was Alice coming to my rescue. I loved the way she talked to me and told me what a good boy I was. If I could have spoken, I would have told her how much I cared for her. Although she was a bit older than the usual females I fantasize about, she ranked high on my list.

CHAPTER 31

Joshua

*The best portion of a good Dog's life,
is his little nameless, unremembered acts
of kindness and love.*

—William Wordsworth and Shiloh

With its beautiful colors, sun-drenched days, and cold nights, fall had arrived. On one of these beautiful days, Jerry received a difficult call from the Wings of Hope Hospice in Allegan, Michigan, asking if we would be willing to travel approximately fifty miles to visit a life-threatened ten-year old boy named Joshua. We were told that Joshua loved Dogs, and he didn't have long to live. I heard Jerry say, "We'll go."

Now is a good time to mention that my master tends to give me all of the credit for my service with the life-threatened. However, he is as soft-hearted and compassionate as I am. We've learned a lot from each other.

We drove the long distance and arrived at the boy's home. When we entered, I counted eighteen noses in the main room.

On a bed lay a very sick young boy whose eyes sparkled when I put my nose up to his hand. We stayed for twenty minutes while I did my usual thing, walking around the room for people to pet me and shake my paw. I care deeply and unconditionally about everyone. I even picked up my leash, because I'm a retriever and that's what I do.

After making the rounds of the room, I went back to Joshua's bedside. He asked Jerry why I was named Shiloh. Jerry explained that it was a biblical name. Before he could continue, Joshua politely interrupted him and said, "Yes, I'm familiar with Genesis and the Old Testament and the coming of the peacemaker, Shiloh."

For a moment, Jerry was unable to speak. This was quite unusual for my master, as he always had a multitude of words to use in any given situation. He regained his composure and said, "Shiloh and I loved meeting you, Joshua."

Joshua responded with, "Thank you, Mr. Hill, for bringing your beautiful Dog to me. I want to ask you a favor."

"Anything, Joshua," said Jerry.

"If I'm still here in a few days, will you bring Shiloh back to visit me?"

"Of course, Joshua."

"If I'm not here it just means I've gone on to heaven to help prepare a place for you and Shiloh in the future."

Jerry was again uncharacteristically quiet. We said our goodbyes as I wagged my tail.

We got into the car, but my master didn't start the engine. Suddenly he said, "Shiloh, forward," which meant that he wanted me to come as close as possible to him. He gave me a big hug and kiss and began to sob. I understood why he was crying. I was in tune with what was happening.

The next day Jerry got a call from the hospice, thanking us for our visit. They said that they would call back when it was a good time for a return visit with Joshua. But when the next call came, it was to tell us that Joshua had already left for heaven.

CHAPTER 32

My New Winter Home

A Dog is an endless source of pleasure.

—Unknown

I was excited and also a bit apprehensive. We were loading up the car to go see our newly purchased condo in Stuart, Florida.

My concern was two-fold: First, I was concerned because we would be towing a U-Haul trailer filled to the brim with our possessions, which meant that instead of seeing cars passing and honking at me, I would be looking backwards at a box on wheels following behind us for thirteen-hundred miles. Little did I know that a bumper sticker on the rear of the car said, "Honk if Ufer Meechigan." Bob Ufer had been the great University of Michigan football announcer. He was football's answer to baseball's Harry Carey. Bob always pronounced Michigan, "Meechigan." Cars overtook us, and if they happened to be University of Michigan fans, they would honk out of respect for Mr. Ufer, who had long ago announced his last Meechigan touchdown and was having his victory celebration upstairs. And here I thought all the honking was about me.

My second worry was about the sharks that roam the ocean just off the south Florida beaches. As I described earlier, Jerry had always given me baths in Lake Michigan and I worried that in Florida I would be taking baths with the sharks.

I was sleeping and dreaming of Jonah and the whale when Jerry stopped the car and issued his familiar order in the style of a navy officer: "Now hear this. Everyone out for a pee. We'll be on the road again in ten minutes."

I've always wondered if Willie Nelson travels this way, spending ten minutes at a pit stop before getting back on the road, again.

It was raining and I don't do my business in the rain. This provoked my master to once again repeat to Barb, "If they ever do Dog-to-human bladder transplants, I want Shiloh's bladder."

I fell back asleep and found myself dreaming about the Indian who drank one hundred cups of tea and drowned in his teepee. I wonder, do humans have weird dreams too, or is it just me?

After two long days and nights, we arrived at our new digs. It was small but I liked it.

We spent the next few days busily buying things that we needed but hadn't crammed into the U-Haul.

We did have time for three walks a day. Most of the time I was on a leash because this was the law in Martin County, but it sure cramped my style. Jerry is a big believer in a Dog's freedom to explore and sniff. I'm a prolific marker with my whizzes, and I usually have free range.

Other than the leash law, I thought I would adapt to my new status very well, spending five months out of the year as a Gator Dog.

CHAPTER 33

Beer and Bones

*If you think Dogs can't count, try putting two biscuits
in your pocket and giving me only one of them.*

—Shiloh

It seemed like every day on our walks we met new people, and more importantly for me, we met new Dogs. I began to realize what Barb meant when she described the purchase of our new condo as an expensive Dog Kennel. Our development, The Indian River Plantation, was very Dog friendly because it allowed property owners to have Dogs. Also, the stretch of the Atlantic Ocean beach that we walked along every day allowed for Dogs on leashes.

Poop bag was a new term to me, and I soon learned its meaning. Jerry, always thinking, taught me early on to do my business in the sea oats that grow between the bank and the sandy beach. People were prohibited from walking in the sea oats, so we weren't required to clean up after me.

It reminded me of Lake Michigan, where the bank met the beach. That spot was called the towline and as the big lake receded from its high water mark of the 1980s, dune grass began to grow there. In my lifetime, all I have known are the dune grasses of Lake Michigan and the sea oats of the Atlantic Ocean. My special fertilizing plan helped this vegetation flourish.

I thought I had met most of the neighboring Dogs, but then a highlight occurred. We were invited to an event called Beer and Bones. Jerry went for beer and I went for bones, which was a great match. This event was held every Sunday from 4:00 to 5:00 p.m. at the Tiki Bar, which was part of the Marriott Hotel on the beach near our condo. It had to be held after the food service was over for the day, and within minutes after 4:00 p.m., Dogs and their masters flocked to this Mecca. The dogs I saw there included a Collie, a German shepherd, a Yorkie, a sheltie, an English setter, a huge Newfie, two Labs, a miniature Australian Shepherd named Tory (one of my favorites), and the winners, six golden retrievers. As I looked over the various owners, it became apparent that many Dogs and their masters resemble each other. I quickly glanced at my master and decided that we didn't resemble each other. For starters, he has blue eyes and a bigger nose.

The event began with lots of sniffing among the Dogs and streams of conversation between Masters. Then came the beer and the bones. I was especially excited on my first visit, as I imagined what might be on the menu: beef bones, soup bones, pork rib bones, and maybe buffalo bones. Unfortunately, this wasn't the case. Dog biscuits were the only menu item available, and it was the same thing every week. I tried to get a protest going for real bones, but the Dog biscuits were just tasty enough that the protest never took off. My next idea was a written petition drive to change the name of the event to Beer and Biscuits, but not many Dogs could hold a pen between their toes. Beer and Bones was a great meeting and eating place for a few years, until some policymaker scuttled the program. I wanted to communicate a Dog's position to Mr. Marriott, but this would have been to no avail, so stale beer, buried bones, and good memories are all that remain.

CHAPTER 34

Carson's Tavern

Good food, good drink, and me under the table,
that's what I call a good tavern.

—Shiloh

Carson's Tavern was a giant step up from Beer and Bones. Barb and Jerry, along with Jerry's college roommate Thorny and his wife Mary, discovered Carson's Tavern one Saturday evening when their reservation at a nearby restaurant was not honored. Not wanting to be discouraged, they walked next door to Carson's.

It was very busy, but there was one table outside that was empty. They asked a young man if they would get service if they stayed. With a knowing smile, he said, "Guaranteed." Within thirty seconds, a server named Danielle was taking the drink order. Their dinner arrived in a timely manner and it was delicious.

After dinner they sought out the manager, who happened to be the same young man they talked to earlier. He turned out to also be the owner. After many compliments on the food service, Mary, a retired Physical Therapist, asked Carson about his missing left arm.

"From birth," he responded.

"Would there be any problem with me bringing my registered therapy Dog on our next visit if we eat outside?" Jerry asked.

"Inside or out, it's no problem. I'd like to meet him," Carson said.

A week later, the five of us returned to Carson's. I met him and instantly I knew that we were going to be good friends. I think it's funny how Dogs sense connections like this before humans do.

Carson's became our favorite watering hole and I always got to go along, including the time I went to Thorny's birthday party in March, which attracted nearly a dozen guests.

I haven't told you yet about Carson's good friend, who was called Joe the Pro. He worked at the Ocean Club Golf Course at the Indian River Plantation. He started as a bag boy and worked his way to the top, and he continues to outwork everyone. His story contains some good lessons about working hard and succeeding. He organizes and runs events and gatherings such as Men's Day, Woman's Day, auctions, tournaments, shootouts, and the famous Ryder Cup. Sometimes Joe and Jerry play golf together and they've become good friends.

One day, Joe invited Jerry, who was a basketball player in his day, to come to the Y-Center and watch the team from Carson's Tavern play. Joe was on the team and when my master and I arrived at the Y to watch them, Carson, with only one arm, was completely outplaying his defender. When Jerry told Joe how impressed he was with Carson's basketball prowess, Joe responded, "You ought to see him play golf!"

After this, they began to hold an annual outing with Carson, who always outplays everyone in the foursome.

A few years later, something traumatic occurred in Jerry's life, which brought Carson and Jerry's relationship to a new level.

In the meanwhile, Kalyn, Krystal and Sarah became our regular servers, and Carson's regular customers were always introducing me to new friends. Although nobody was officially allowed to feed me, it always seemed that a few morsels made it from the table to the floor.

I was part of some large dinner groups, and I always responded to my master's voice command, "Shiloh, Sit," and then, "Shiloh, under the table." Once settled under the table, and Jerry is drinking his second draft beer, I always move slowly through the maze of feet and legs, shredding a paper napkin along the way, until I find my friend Thorny. Although everyone has been warned over and over, "Don't feed Shiloh," Thorny has perfected his ability to look people in the eye while doling out freebies to me under the table. Fortunately for me, my master has given up on his no food rule with his old college buddy, Thorny. He and I have remained good friends with our secret feeding arrangement.

CHAPTER 35

Chewed Out

When we hold our tongues and listen,
we communicate our care
for an open ear speaks volumes
to a heart that's in despair.

—Sper

I t's been a few chapters since I've talked about my therapy work. Let me tell you about an incident that happened in Florida early one Wednesday morning. I was on my normal trek to the beach when my master unhooked my leash and uttered two of my favorite words, "Shiloh, beach!"

With no one around during this time of day, this was our normal procedure, but on this particular day, a woman's shrill voice screamed from a balcony above, "Get that damn Dog on a leash. It's the law of Martin County and I can have you arrested!"

We were both stunned by her anger over this transgression, and although I sensed that Jerry was fuming, he calmly said, "You're right, ma'am. I'm sorry. He's a Therapy Dog and he needs his freedom to run before he does his volunteer work today."

She shrieked, "I don't give a tinkers damn what he is, you're both breaking the law and in deep trouble."

At that point, I thought I saw smoke coming out of Jerry's ears, but he calmly said, "You're right, he's back on his leash."

She had been standing on a second floor balcony, and although neither of us had seen her before, she had a face that I would never forget.

When we reached the beach, my master kept me on my leash and said, "Sorry, ole fella, we'll go along with the law today. She's having a terrible day and it's got nothing to do with either of us. She just needed to vent her frustration."

Although I didn't understand his words, I got his drift. I got to sniff a lot of things as I took care of my morning business. I didn't have as much freedom on a leash, but it wasn't that bad.

When we returned home, Jerry left for his Men's Day golfing event. He left the sliding door open so that I could go out onto the porch and watch him come through on hole number ten, which was about the distance of a pitching wedge from our condo's porch. I had already forgotten about the irate woman, and I fell asleep on the porch dreaming about one of our favorite activities. Half an hour before sunset, my master would take me, along with a bag of shag balls, to the tenth green, and I would lay down and watch while he chipped and putted. We were both careful not to tip over his beer can next to the green. Sometime later, I woke up to find that the regular Florida foursome of Bob, Tom, Gary, and Jerry were below me on the green putting. From their conversation I surmised that Jerry had to make an eight-foot putt for a much needed birdie for the team.

Although he couldn't hear me, I muttered to myself as a way of giving instructions to Jerry: "Keep your head still. You pulled it to the left again. Obviously more putting practice is needed."

I fell back asleep and had a surfing dream, and this one was inspired by a national news story about a surfing Dog. In this dream, I broke all of the competitive records and was mobbed by bikini-clad coeds when I hit the beach. It was a lovely dream, but I was awakened from it by the twins, Karen and Sharon, who came to the condo every two weeks to help Barb with the cleaning. They're a bit older than coeds, but they're awfully nice and I still can't tell them apart. Jerry came home and said, "Shiloh, you've got work to do."

Then we left to go to the Treasure Coast Hospice. As is the normal routine, we checked in at the nurses' station. On that day they gave us assignments for rooms three, five, six, and eight. We knocked lightly on the first door and Jerry announced that I was is in the building and available for a visit. On this day, rooms three and five said yes to my visit and room six was sound asleep.

We announced ourselves at room eight, and a woman said brusquely, "No, go away."

We heard another woman say, "Mom, Dad loves Dogs. Let them in."

With that invitation, we entered the room and I moved toward the man's bed. He was weak but very friendly, and he petted me for a long time. I then went to the daughter and her husband. They too were very nice and good at petting. After one more visit to the gentleman in the bed, we said our goodbyes.

As we left, the older woman stepped out into the hallway with us. She said to my master, "You look so familiar, I'm sure we've met but I can't think of where."

He hesitated, considered telling her, and said, "I'm not sure. It could be Shiloh you've met, although golden retrievers are all so similar in their looks." Then we left.

Once outside, my master said, "Shy, the world is full of problems and challenges. This morning we were challenged with someone else's problem. Fortunately, we didn't let our natural reaction show, and by absorbing her ranting and raving, her frustration was somewhat alleviated. Just now you helped a dying man, as well as his daughter and son-in-law, have a few moments of golden pleasure. Maybe you gave his wife a bit of help, too. Let's hope she never remembers where she first met us."

CHAPTER 36

Alzheimer's

> *Did you ever walk into a room and forget*
> *why you walked in? I think that's how we Dogs spend our lives.*
>
> —Shiloh

Later on, I'll tell you about my first visit to a church, but for now I want to share with you one of my more interesting volunteer activities.

In the back of our church building there's an Alzheimer's daycare service that meets five days a week, from 10:00 a.m. to 5:00 p.m. Jerry and I visit weekly and stay for thirty minutes. When I arrive everyone gets quite excited, and Teresa, the person in charge, introduces me.

All I really know about Alzheimer's is that the people who have it are really friendly and they talk incessantly. Every time I see them it's like they've never seen me before, even though I come every week. I remember them by shape, smell, and sight, but they always act like it is the first time

I've visited them. But this really doesn't matter, and I serve them unconditionally as they repeatedly ask my master my name. He respectfully answers and sometimes he asks if they had Dogs when they grew up. They will respond with every detail about their childhood dogs, including its name, breed, and how old they were when they had them. They often tell stories about how their Dogs left this earth through illnesses, car accidents, or running away. While telling these stories, they continually ask Jerry about my name and age. I'm amazed at how they are able to maintain detailed and accurate long-term recollections despite the loss of their short-term memory.

Apparently this is what happens when people develop this condition. The staff informed Jerry that encouraging these Alzheimer's patients to talk about their lives is a therapeutic and stimulating interaction for them. I'm just happy that my presence is helpful.

Before we left, I revisited the room one last time, in case anyone wants to pet me or have another word with me. One of the elderly women caressed my coat and murmured soft endearments in my ear. She seemed to be calling me by another name, but I sensed that it was probably the name of a Dog she had earlier in her life. Another woman took a brush that Jerry brought and groomed me, making my coat shiny with her stokes.

I looked forward to the next week's visit, knowing that it would be like going on their stage for the first time. I thought that maybe I did understand them. One of my favorite sayings is, "A Dog with a short memory is a Dog with a clear conscience."

CHAPTER 37

Auntie E

My wagging tail tells how happy I am to see you.
—Shiloh

Shortly after returning to Michigan from Florida, we visited Aunt Ethel, or Auntie E as everyone called her. She had inspired Jerry to have me become a Therapy Dog, and I loved her for that. When we first met, I was a puppy and she was ninety-eight years young. When I saw her this time, I was six years old and in my prime. She had always been very lucid and attractive for her age.

The second to last time we saw her, Aunt Ethel was getting her hair done at the retirement home salon. It was in December and we were about to leave for Florida. We found her in the salon and her head was tilted back while the beautician worked her magic on her hair. She couldn't see us, so Jerry announced, "Auntie E, Merry Christmas a few weeks early! I left your present in your room."

She responded, "That's nice of you and Barb, but at my age, one hundred four, your friendship and visits are your best gifts. Is Shiloh here?"

"Yep," Jerry said as he guided her hand so that she was touching my head. She had the most loving touch. I always welcomed her caresses.

After her hair appointment was over, we wheeled her back to her room. She looked great. Auntie E had been married twice, and while she had no children, she did have a zillion nieces, nephews, grandnieces, and grandnephews. She was the only girl in a large family, of which Jerry's dad was the oldest. They were born in the Upper Peninsula of Michigan, where their dad was the engineer of the local tannery. He reportedly brought the first car, a 1906 Orient Buckboard, to the Upper Peninsula. He never found a buyer and eventually had to ship it back downstate. Despite being born in 1874 and raising a large family, their mother lived to be 107 ½ years old. Her sister, Dill, made it to 101, and her brother Tom lived to 107. When I heard this story, I felt much younger than the 7:1 ratio normally applied to Dogs. At 104, Auntie E seemed much younger than her years because she was so vibrant and full of life.

She looked great when we saw her that time in December, but when we visited her in May, she looked and seemed her age. She seemed to have aged immensely in the six months since we had seen her last. When she petted me, her usual warm touch seemed very cold. I was worried, but I didn't know what to do with my feelings. I sensed that her final transition wasn't too far off.

A few weeks later, Jerry received a call that Auntie E had slipped into a coma. We hurriedly drove to Jackson.

She lay on her back on her bed and looked more like a wax figure from Madame Trousseau's Museum than our beloved Auntie E. Jerry pulled up a chair next to the bed, put his hand on hers, and told her how much he loved her. I liked to hear that. Then Jerry pulled me close and put my paw on her hand. I backed off in embarrassment. Jerry and I looked into each other's eyes. We both knew what this meant.

When we left, Jerry asked the nurse, "How long?"

"Could be days or even a week. It's hard to say."

"I don't think she'll make it through the night," he said.

The nurse seemed unimpressed with his projection.

It took two hours to return to the lake house. Barb gave Jerry a hug and said, "Sorry, they called and Auntie E died shortly after you and Shiloh left."

Jerry got down on the floor and gave me a hug and cried. Everyone loved Auntie E.

A few days later, Aunt Ethel's minister called and asked if Barb and Jerry would bring me to the funeral.

Throughout the service, I laid on the floor in the front, near the minister. During his eulogy, he talked about Aunt Ethel's relationship with a special Therapy Dog named Shiloh.

She was one of the really good humans in the world and she'll be sorely missed.

CHAPTER 38

Four Eyes

Nobody is old and nobody
wears glasses.

—Heaven is for Real Todd Burpo

I like to look Dogs and humans right in the eye. Dogs are like people in that if they look you in the eye, you can usually trust them. If they look everywhere but at you, my experience suggests that they're shifty and possibly untrustworthy. When I encounter a human who will not look me in the eye, I try to stay away from that person. This could spell trouble for me. This means that they obviously don't like Dogs and they might even fear them.

I've never seen a Dog with glasses, but many humans wear them and their four eyes confuse me, so I use my best sense and try to sniff out their sincerity.

As Woodrow Wilson once said, "If a Dog will not come to you after having looked you in the face, you should go home and examine your conscience."

Some people let their glasses slide down their noses and peer over them at whatever they are focusing on. I couldn't understand why people wear them if they aren't going to use them properly, but my master said that these people usually only need them to read or look at something closely. They don't need to look through the lenses to see things in the distance. I've come to understand that people's vision deteriorates as they age, just as a Dog's vision does. But when Dogs are young and frisky, they can spot a deer in the woods several hundred yards away. Humans do not have this facility. Of course, I sense the deer first, then I smell it, and then I see it.

When I meet a new Dog, I also look to see how he or she holds their head. Even when they are barking, by holding their heads high Dogs let me know that they are friendly. The Dog that lowers his head and growls can't be trusted, so look out.

The wagging of a Dog's tail is another signal. If a Dog is barking but wagging his tail, he more than likely is friendly. However, if he is not wagging his tail, his bark may be a warning to stay away.

Pay attention to the visual interaction between a Dog and its master. Unlike wolves, which avoid eye contact, Dogs search their master's faces for clues about their emotions, and they react accordingly.

Sometimes I go into unfamiliar surroundings, which makes me nervous on occasion. I gauge my safety by watching my master's face. His face always reassures me that no harm will befall me.

My master says that it's very satisfying when he gazes into my eyes. I return his look with what he refers to as my big, beautiful brown eyes. Since I mentioned my ancestors, the wolves, I'll tell you more about them later in the book.

Whether you're a Dog or a human, you should be using your eyes to look at the wonderful world around us. You might see a great blue heron hunting at the edge of a quiet lake, a clump of delicate spring wild flowers carpeting a wooden slope, or the wetlands of a nature preserve. Look and see. Enjoy the beauty of our world.

There is sadness and pain in the world too, and we shouldn't deny this. My master tells me that the weight of a burden a human must sometimes carry will never exceed his or her ability to carry it.

CHAPTER 39

Sara's School

I Love KIDS

—Shiloh

n the spring, I was invited to a special place. Every spring, just prior to summer vacation, I go to the Glenn, Michigan Elementary School to educate the kindergarteners and the first and second graders. My master talks to them about the role of Dogs in society.

Jerry calls it The Dog and Pony Show. Since I'm the Dog, he must be the pony. After a wonderfully flattering introduction by the teacher, Ms. Jones, I walk around the room, visiting each child at their desk. They pet me, shake my paw, and sometimes they give me a hug or two before we begin the presentation. I lie in the middle of the room while Jerry drones on about my amazing resume of volunteerism. He then asks the KIDS if they know of any other ways in which Dogs help people. Some of their answers are incredible. For example, one of the children talked about the Dog who leads blind KIDS across a busy street so that the cars won't scare them. Another child mentioned the talking Dog, which I will tell you about in chapter 66. One little girl mentioned how Dogs that have been in a particular family for years often take on the responsibility of keeping the young children safe. In an unfamiliar space, like the woods or a field or the beach, Dogs will herd the kids like they would cattle or sheep to direct them away from danger.

Jerry points out to the children that studies have shown that elderly people live longer when they have a Dog in the home. And Dogs are being trained these days to help physically challenged people prepare meals, get things out of the cupboard or medicine cabinet, and do all sorts of daily chores that the person could not do by themselves.

When Jerry's discussion time is over, it is time for the KIDS to go crazy throwing the tennis ball around. The children perform simple throws and catches with a bouncing ball, which I handle easily. One time an incident occurred that we refer to as the coup de grâce. My master bounced a ball off of the top of a desk and I fielded it on the fly. Wild applause erupted. I was the hero of the day. The children clamored around me to give me hugs and praises. Of course, I loved every minute of it.

One time Jerry let a little girl named Mary toss the ball. Her throw went backwards and the teacher jumped and made a great catch. Having watched a lot of basketball on TV, I wished that I could jump and dunk.

Sara, age six, came to our side and asked me for a paw autograph. Jerry dropped to his knees, puts Sara's pencil between my toes and we wrote, "To Sara. Have a great summer, Love and Licks, Shiloh."

Then more of the children surrounded me and asked for my autograph. Jerry patiently made sure that each one of them received a personal note signed by yours truly.

I really liked the teacher Ms. Jones. She was quite young and pretty and she loved her students. Educating them to the best of her ability is a high priority for her. I am one of her favorites too. She always greets me with, "Shiloh, I'm so happy to see you again. Welcome to our classroom." I always have a great time at the Glenn Elementary School.

CHAPTER 40

A Day At The Museum

Study your local history.

—Professor Shiloh

Every summer I stay very busy on Fridays. Jerry and I go to the Hospice of Holland at 9:00 a.m. and we visit patients from 9:30 a.m. until 11:00 a.m. We say goodbye to the staff, especially Dr. Roger, and our next stop is the Saugatuck-Douglas Historical Museum (sdhistoricalsociety.org) on the Kalamazoo River.

I usually lay outside, looking out at the beautiful Kalamazoo River, which winds its way to Lake Michigan. Taking my own advice from a previous chapter, when I talked about using your eyes, I drink in all of the beautiful scenery, including the flower gardens, the birds flying overhead, and the fish jumping high in the wake of the Star of Saugatuck excursion boat, which leaves from its mooring directly across from the museum.

Every hour the duck boat floats by. This amphibious vehicle, which begins its tours on the streets of Saugatuck, drives like a truck until it enters the Kalamazoo Lake then goes into the river before returning onto terra firma.

Both the duck's captain and the Star of Saugatuck give our museum some free publicity by loudspeaker when passing down river. Sometimes they point out me: Shiloh, the Museum Dog. Of course, I love this attention.

While I watch the activity on the river, my Master prepares the museum for its noon opening.

The museum is small but fascinating. The amazing history of the area is well displayed. An interactive computer explains the history with slide shows and a new exhibit is presented each year.

For example, one year the exhibit highlighted the Big Pavilion, once called the brightest spot on the Great Lakes. Opening in 1909, it contained a huge dance hall, restaurant, movie theaters, and a bowling alley. During the 1940s, many of the big dance bands played there. Jerry often tells visitors about how he and his friends at the University of Michigan used to take breaks from finals to travel from Ann Arbor to Saugatuck. They would stop at the Big Pavilion to meet girls and dance. Unfortunately, the brightest spot on the Great Lakes went up in a blazing inferno in 1960.

Younger children aren't too interested in the museum, so I become their entertainment, allowing their parents and grandparents to enjoy the unique exhibits. Sometimes a friend named Donna would volunteer with us and she was great at explaining all of the books and ringing up sales.

Since the museum is located near the 302 stairs to the top of Oval Mountain, or Mount Baldy, we sell lots of water and t-shirts with "I Climbed Mount Baldy" printed on the front.

At 4:00 p.m. we close up, put everything away, and head home to Barb at the lake house, having fulfilled another successful day of volunteering.

CHAPTER 41

Pup – Pup – Pup

Call me anything, just call me.

—Shiloh

When I was a small Dog, Jerry called me pup and it seemed natural. However, I'm now an old Dog and he still calls me pup.

Let's examine this. My first theory is that he feels I'm still part wolf. Lupomorphism is the belief that Dogs are much like wolves and should be handled accordingly. Therefore I'm what is called a pup in the pack. Sometimes I dream that I'm a wolf and that I evolved into the wonderful, sweet, intelligent Dog that I am today. I dream that only my master knows about my awful secret and he will tell no one as long as I behave. It does make me a bit nervous, his knowing smile as he calls me pup. Dogs and wolves communicate with their eyes, ears, tails, and posture.

If Jerry had a tail, I'd think he was part wolf and that we were related.

My second theory is that Jerry calls all his grandkids pup, which makes it a term of love and endearment. When we meet small children on our walks, they also become part of the pack and he calls them pup too.

With the name like Shiloh, people often tell me, "Oh, you're named for the Civil War battle in Tennessee." These people probably don't read the Bible. Sometimes these same people say that I'm a "nice girl." I accept this as nothing personal. They probably had female Dogs all of their lives and they don't usually drop to the ground to examine my underside. Sometimes people refer to me as a "girl magnet," as I do attract a good many good-lookers, as you'll read later.

I am curious about many masters who refer to their Dogs by names such as, Sweetie Girl, Buddy Boy, Friend, Dog, Hey You, Whizzer (I have gotten that), Chow Hound, Pooper (yuk), Youngster, Oldster, Rover, Mutt, and Heinz 57. In my vast experience, a real Heinz 57 is usually an exceptionally good representative of the canine fraternity.

When I approach strangers with my wagging tail and friendly demeanor, they'll ask, "What's your Dog's name?" With a twinkle in his eye, Jerry answers, "Shy-low, but he should be called Bold-high!" He has an interesting answer or comment for most everything. When it comes to my master calling me names, my favorite is, "Love ya pup!"

CHAPTER 42
Banned From the Pump House

You can't see a rainbow with your back to it.

—Shiloh

O ver the years, my master has been a fiend for exercising. My favorite way of exercising is to walk along the beaches of Florida and Michigan, climbing lots of stairs and swimming in Lake Michigan.

This is not enough for Jerry, so when we are in Saugatuck, we go on a regular basis to the Pump House Gym. Guy and Sister Nita own and run the establishment. Nita's got the perfect name because she's a neat lady. For years everyone welcomed me and I would move from machine to machine as Jerry worked out. I loved the cool concrete floor on my underside, and I would occasionally fall asleep. My dreams would often cause me to moan, groan, and thump my tail. Amid lots of laughter, some Pump House guys would wake me up to tell me that Jerry was done and he was leaving. I would stretch and sniff, accepting a few hugs and pets, and stopping by the front desk so that neat Nita could say, "Bye Shy."

This was the regular routine until one fateful day. Everything seemed fine at first. I had walked several times between the machines that Jerry was working out on, when I spotted a fellow I'd never seen before. He was rather flabby and rotund, and he certainly needed to work out. As the self-appointed Pump House Ambassador, I sauntered over and placed my nose gently in his lap as my way of saying hello. He was working out on a machine, pushing weights up with both of his arms and hands. Since he was looking up, he hadn't realized that I was there and that my nose was touching. When I pushed my nose firmly between his flabby legs, he catapulted straight up into the air as the weights came down. This was a bad decision on my part. I stood back and watched as he shouted in pain and horror. Then he saw me for the first time. "Get that damn Dog out of here!" he yelled.

My master was at my side immediately, apologizing and explaining that I was a licensed Therapy Dog and that I meant him no harm. But as we looked at him, we both realized that I had caused him harm. I was hurriedly led outside and we left.

The next day, Nita called to say that I was no longer the Pump House Ambassador. My master continued to work out there, but only on days that were cool enough for me to remain in the car.

Everywhere we go in the Saugatuck area, people say, "Shiloh, we've missed you at the Pump House and we're worried about whether you were still on the top side of the green grass. It's good to see you."

The underside of the green grass sounds very spooky to me. I can't imagine peeing up instead of down.

Jerry has grown tired of telling the story of Shiloh, the flabby man, and my expulsion from the gym. Instead, my master simply thanks people for their concern.

Flabby never returned to the Pump House, even though he sorely needed to exercise. I was very sorry about that little adventure.

CHAPTER 43

Uncle Jack

The Dog is a gentleman
I hope to go to his heaven, not man's.

—Mark Twain

J erry had one brother, Jack, who lived a remarkable life, having survived for sixteen years after receiving a heart transplant. He was bigger than life, and it was easy to see where my master got his gift of gab. When Jerry and Jack were in a room together there was never a dull moment.

Uncle Jack, as he was called, loved to play golf, and he and Jerry would sometimes go to Mark's golf course near Kalkaska to play. The first time they played together, I jumped into my usual spot next to Jerry in the golf cart and waited for Jack to sit next to me. Jack wasn't used to the pairing of humans and dogs in a golf cart, and he made this clear to his brother.

"Jerry, what is Shiloh doing in the cart?" he asked incredulously.

"He always rides with me, Jack. Where else would he go?" Jerry replied with a smile.

Jack thought that it would be better for me to stay at the golf shop or in the car or back at the hunting cabin while they were golfing, but Jerry would have none of that. Jack had always owned little Dogs, mostly Schnauzers, so I guess he just wasn't used to a big Dog like me.

Whenever they played together, Jerry and I drove in one cart and Jack had one to himself. It was probably better that way, as Jack hit everything short but down the middle of the fairway. Jerry and I would have to search in the woods a few times every round for one of his balls.

As time went on, Jack's health deteriorated enough so that he and Jerry could no longer play golf together. But he would still make trips to the family cabin where he and my master shared a bedroom. Jack hadn't realized that I slept on his bed when he wasn't at the cabin. One night when he came to bed he saw me curled up in his sleeping bag.

"Jerry, if I'm not going to sit with Shiloh in a golf cart, I'm certainly not going to sleep with him!" Jack said laughing.

So I decided I'd better let him have his bed and lay down at the end of my master's bed. It was a tight fit, as with the golf cart, but I didn't like being far from my master so we made it work. If either of the brothers started snoring too loudly, I'd jump down and go sleep on the couch near the fireplace.

We visited Jack and his wife Ellie in Jackson, Michigan, occasionally. Their Dog Heidi was a yapper, and being a schnauzer, she had that small Dog's issue of trying to scare big Dogs. I took it all in stride. I would go to her pile of toys, pick out a squeaky one, and make my own noise until my master said, "Shiloh, enough." As soon as I dropped the toy, Heidi would retrieve it and run underneath the nearest table. She really was a great Dog and she was Jack's special buddy. I liked her in spite of her little Dog issues.

Jack's health started to give out in 2006, so Jerry and I made frequent trips to visit him. On our very last trip, he was slipping in and out of consciousness. I nudged his hand and he barely murmured, "Hi, Shiloh."

Jerry decided that this was finally the time for me to share a bed with Jack, so he lifted me up and put me down next to his brother. Jack put his gentle hand on top of my head, which let me know that he was okay with me being by his side this one final time.

CHAPTER 44

That Damn Dog

*Dogs never talk about themselves but listen
to you while you talk about yourself and keep
up an appearance of being interested in the
conversation.*

—Jerome K. Jerome

For several years I made visits to the Inn at Freedom Village in Holland, Michigan. My favorite friend to visit was Joe. He was in his late eighties when we first met through his daughter, Eva.

On my first visit he was a bit reserved and stuffy. He was dressed in a three-piece herringbone suit, sitting in a recliner chair and reading the Wall Street Journal. His one-room apartment was full of pictures from his career as a lawyer. I didn't receive any warm or fuzzy feelings from him, but I decided to give the relationship my best shot. I nuzzled him with my nose and his response was, "Whose damn

Dog is this?" His comment upset me but my master quickly intervened and explained, "Eva sent us." This seemed to qualify me as being okay.

He only wanted to talk about current world affairs and he paid no attention to me. I snoozed while the men worked on solving global problems.

On our next visit, Joe's opening comment was, "Where ya been? Thought you'd be back sooner." Joe actually ruffled my hair and referred to me as "a good damn Dog." Over the next few years, I became fond of Joe and his greeting of "that damn Dog." He always talked about the latest news and gave his opinions freely. He referred to me as a "damn good listener."

Then we had a new reason to visit Freedom Village. Barb was rehabilitating after surgery, and she was there on two different occasions over a two-year period. At mealtime she sat at a table for four, including a one-hundred-year-old lady. Eventually the lady became a hospice patient and I visited her until she passed away. On her table she kept a picture of me, as well as a newspaper article about me. She couldn't speak words anymore, but she would make happy purring sounds while she petted my head.

We were at the lake house one day when I heard Jerry exclaim, "We'll come now." Eva had called to say that Joe had slipped into a coma, and he had been given only a short time to live. When we arrived Jerry gave Eva a hug and Eva gave me one. We went to Joe's bedside and Jerry placed Joe's hand on my head. Within seconds, Joe's eyes opened briefly and he muttered clearly, "that damn Dog."

He closed his eyes and my friend was gone.

CHAPTER 45

If I Can Jump It, We'll Buy It

Never underestimate yourself.

—Shiloh

Jerry and I went back to Twin Birch, Mark's golf course in northern Michigan. Bob, Jerry M., and Tom were meeting us for golf followed by lunch at Birdie's Pub. Birdie's Pub, the restaurant at the golf course that Mark had named after his great golden retriever, Birdie, whose life both Mark and Jerry had shared for sixteen years. I always felt that I must show reverence when being in my predecessor's namesake restaurant. After a cup of coffee and donuts, we were off to the first tee.

Mark had just driven up and Jerry asked, "Son, where's your car?"

"Long story, Dad. I'll bring you up-to-date after your golf round."

When we had finished a fun round on a neat course, we hit Birdie's Pub for beer and brats. I went under the table and faced the fake, talking deer-head that was mounted on the wall. It bugged me, especially when it started singing, 'On the Road Again' by Willie Nelson. It seemed awfully real when the head moved up and down and side to side.

Mark knew how to entertain kids when they ate in his restaurant with their families. He had a remote control that he could operate out of sight, and when a kid would approach the mounted deer head, he would push a button that would make the deer start to talk. The talking deer head had a dozen different songs and sayings, but my favorite was, "Never trust a hunter with a gun. Look where I ended up?"

Mark came to our table and quizzed us about our golf round. Then he told Jerry his car story. With 175,000 miles on it, his car had bitten the dust, and he was driving a rental car daily for the sixty-mile round trip from Traverse City.

Jerry, ever the spontaneous dad, said, "Son, would you like my Bravada? It's got 100,000 miles on it, but it runs like a top."

"Sure, but what would you drive?"

My master turned to Bob and asked when he was getting his new Chevrolet Suburban truck?

"In a couple of months," Bob replied.

"Why don't I buy your old Suburban and you drive your Jeep until your new wheels arrive?" he asked, ever the wheeler-dealer.

Bob agreed and the negotiations were under way.

Jerry put one qualifying condition to the deal. "If Shiloh can jump it, we'll buy it."

When we went outside, they opened the back door, and I effortlessly jumped into the back of the Suburban. Next, I jumped easily over the back gate. It was no problem. The deal was set and we were off in our new used Suburban with only 18,000 miles on it. Bob got a ride with Jerry M. back to his north woods cabin.

Mark was ecstatic. Bob had a nice check in his pocket, and Jerry was smiling. I was happy that I still had good jumping muscles.

CHAPTER 46

Missy and Me

A Dog is girl's best friend.

—Shiloh

Missy and I have been good friends for many years. She lives in Traverse City with Mark, Anne, Carly, and Lindsay. Being a Sheltie, what she lacks in size she more than makes up for in heart.

Missy has always had cats for her best friends, as well as me. At any one time her household will have up to three felines that tease me when I arrive. I just want to play, but when I make the first move they part like the red sea and I end up looking at an empty space. They're used to Missy. Either my size scares them or they are just teasing me. I haven't figured it out yet.

Since they always took their catnaps on the chairs and couches, I assumed that it was okay for me to do likewise. I was wrong. Anne came home from work one day while I was snuggled between several throw pillows on the big divan and interrupted my dream. I was ushered unceremoniously to the back desk and put on a long leash. I felt imprisoned until Mark arrived and gave me an early release.

I travel to Traverse City a few times every year and spend a lot of playtime in Missy's backyard. Whenever someone throws a tennis ball for her to retrieve for an entire hour, she looks very disappointed when they say, "Enough, Missy."

I learned a long time ago that I couldn't outrun Missy, so I would wait for her to run past the ball and then I would get it. We're the same age but I got tired just watching her amazing endurance.

However, when she comes to the lake house it's a different ballgame. We dash down the sixty-one steps to the Lake Michigan beach and wait for our human hurlers to arrive with the tennis balls. I finish a distant second until someone throws the balls into the water. Missy will not even get her feet wet, so I nonchalantly wade in, pick up the wet ball, and purposely pass closely to Missy. This might not be very polite. I'm not perfect. But I almost am. Actually I learned later in life that Dogs with very heavy coats like Missy are sometimes afraid that they will be weighted down if they get wet. Fearing that they would be unable to swim to safety, they avoid the water.

My cousins, the short-haired Labrador retrievers, are ideally suited to be natural waterdogs. We golden retrievers are somewhere in between. We are long-haired but our fur is not heavy enough to cause us concern.

Recently I learned that Missy had some serious health problems. I wish her well, but I realize that both of us are in the twilight of our lives. Like Missy, I just want to be as good of a friend to as many people and Dogs as I can for as long as God allows me to. And of course, I want the companionship of my master, who is my closest friend, for as long as possible.

CHAPTER 47

Shiloh and What's His Name

I've touched so many hearts.

—Shiloh

Almost everywhere I go I'm recognized by name. "Here comes Shiloh. Hey, look. It's the Therapy Dog. Would you like a visit from a hospet Dog?"
This greeting is common and normal at the hospital, as well as the Hospice of Holland and the Treasure Coast Hospice in Florida. I have visited so many people that I am nearly a household name among life-threatened people and their families.

"Here comes Shiloh and what's his name," is a comment that doesn't seem to faze my master. He takes it all in stride. After all, I am the featured attraction and Jerry loves to see me in the limelight.

In Florida and Michigan, I'm recognized for my volunteer work. I've had little kids tell their parents or grandparents that I'm the famous Therapy Dog that helps people. Whether performing at an elementary school, shopping in stores or in a restaurant, kids call me by name and bring others to meet me.

When I'm under a table in a restaurant, children sometimes ask my master if they can pet me. He surveys the restaurant, and if it's not busy and we're not going to create a traffic jam, he'll say that it's okay. If it is busy, he'll ask the children to meet and pet me outside before we leave the area. What's-his-name sometimes tells the children that you can't pet a Service Dog in a restaurant. However, since I'm a Therapy Dog and not working at the time, he'll bend the rules and permit a brief hello. There is a fine line here that I've never understood. It's important, he tells the children, that no matter where you are, you always ask a Dog's master if you can pet their Dog. This applies to Therapy Dogs, Service Dogs, and all other Dogs.

Some people talk about my record of over one thousand hospice visits. They ask, "How many have you done now?" My master gives them the current number, which usually elicits some ohs and ahs. Sometimes people will say, "Have you ever thought of advising the *Guinness Book of Records* on this remarkable achievement?"

I think it's a great idea, but I haven't seen my master send off any letters or emails about this. I think Jerry is content that we are recognized as Shiloh and what's-his-name. And if he is content, then so am I.

CHAPTER 48

Unconditional Love

They do not truly love who do
not show their love.

—Shakespeare

When I give my love to people, I receive love in
return ten-fold through people hugging me,
petting me, and saying that I am such a good
Dog. I love this and it makes my admirers feel good too. I
don't see people as tall or short, heavy or thin, young or old,
healthy or sick, or rich or poor. I just see them as people. I
can often tell when a person is very ill, and I give whatever I
have with no thought of getting anything back. That's what
unconditional love is.

I like what Gilda Radner said: "I think Dogs are the
most amazing creatures. They give unconditional love. For
me, they are the role models for being alive."

Based on my intimate knowledge of Dogs, we are a trusting and loving species of animal that is dependent on humans for love and affection. When we are trained to be Therapy Dogs, we give unconditional love to life-threatened people without hesitation. We instinctively give unconditional love to our owners. We are often unselfish with our human masters and mistresses, sometimes saving them from fires, floods, and other catastrophes. We have been known to travel many miles when lost, in order to return to our families or home territory.

We have been observed to grieve openly when our masters die. The loss of human connections, particularly with the most important people in our lives, can be devastating.

Evidence suggests that Dogs evolved from gray wolves approximately fifteen thousand years ago. Dogs are considered to be the first animals that were domesticated by humans. This domestication began between seventeen thousand and fourteen thousand years ago. When exactly this process began is controversial.

In the early days, wolves lived near human camps because of the reliability of their food source. They were allowed to clean up the scraps and bones around the campfires. As the wolf became domesticated, living in the camps gave them a better chance at breeding with wild wolves. The animals were a great benefit to early man, who used them when they went hunting. This domestication may have been one of the most important factors in human survival.

The evolution from wolf to domesticated pet gradually came about over centuries. Dogs were used to pioneer new lands, guide soldiers during war, and hunt for food. In the present time they are trained to be guide and service Dogs and Therapy Dogs. Once you have the affection and loyalty of a Dog, you will have no better friend. Dogs show their unconditional love to all of the people who are important in their lives.

I'm not sure where love comes from, but according to Jerry it's got something to do with God. Jerry and Barb go to church almost every Sunday when they are in Stuart, Florida, and I occasionally get to go too. I've had some interesting experiences there and I want to share them with you.

CHAPTER 49

My First Church Visit

*Our main job in life is to make life here on earth
a little bit more like heaven.*

—Robert T. Kiyosaki

Minister Randy, the minister at our church in Stuart, has a golden retriever, and Jerry and I instantly bonded with Randy when we discovered that he was a golden man.

One day my master got a call from Randy. I didn't know what they were talking about, but I heard Jerry say, "We'll do it."

The next Sunday Jerry and I went to the church thirty minutes earlier than usual. I heard Jerry say, "The neighbors will bring you, Barb, at the regular time."

I didn't have a clue about what was going on. I had never been to church in my life. I learned later that Randy wanted me to come to church to surprise everyone. I rested between the first and second pews and fell quickly asleep. I dreamed that there were hundreds of people coming into the church and they were singing. The minister was talking in my dream about how everyone can help others by giving them their money, time, and help, and he said that today's sermon would be on benevolence.

Minister Randy said, "People can even give through a wonderful therapy Dog named Shiloh." At that point, Randy asked Jerry to bring me forward.

I awoke with a start and realized that I wasn't dreaming. I was about to go on stage in front of all the parishioners. Jerry had me on heel and took me to the front of the church where Randy greeted me by saying, "Good morning Shiloh."

I instantly sat and offered a paw to Randy, who shook it and laughed aloud. The congregation responded likewise.

Randy went on to explain that I was a special Therapy Dog that had made over one thousand hospice facility visits and went on a regular basis to the local hospital, as well as Alzheimer's care facilities including a day care facility for Alzheimer's in this very church.

Randy continued to tell the congregation that I would be visiting the children in the Sunday school room. "But first," Minister Randy said, "let us pray."

I was quite tired with all of this attention being focused on me, and for some reason I immediately dropped to the floor on all fours and crossed my front paws as we golden retrievers do on occasion. Randy looked down at my prayerful position and he lost it. He began to laugh at the sight of me appearing to be praying. He finally regained his composure and continued the prayer.

After the prayer, I went to Sunday school and entertained the children before they commenced with other activities.

I sometimes dream about poetry and songs. While in Sunday school I wanted somehow to relate my favorite Sunday school song, but I couldn't sing, so my master sang the following song to the children:

Noah was an old man
Who stumbled in the dark
He picked up a hammer
And built himself an ark
He let in the animals, including two Golden Retrievers
Two by two
He thought he had an ark
But he found he had a zoo.

I had to go to the corner and place my paws over my ears because Jerry could not carry a tune, but the children didn't seem to care.

Afterwards, we returned to church, where Randy was giving the sermon. The easiest place to lie was in the aisle next to my master's pew. This time instead of sleeping I listened to the first sermon of my life. Later, I wondered why Jerry hadn't brought me to church earlier. We could all use religion.

After the service was over, Jerry and Barb took me to the recreation room for the coffee social. I heard Minister Randy say that we would have doughnut holes too. I was excited. I'd never had a doughnut hole, but I imagined how delicious they would be.

When we arrived the room was jammed with people. Jerry got his coffee. I still hadn't seen the infamous doughnut holes. My master began to talk to people, which he is well known for, but I still didn't see any doughnut holes.

He introduced me to Dick Gidley, an active church member who was ninety-five years young. Then, two elderly ladies came up and patted me on the top of my head and said, "Mr. Hill, how did you ever teach this beautiful Dog to cross his paws and pray?"

Jerry pointed skyward and said, "Ladies, where are we?"

They looked a bit perplexed and said, "In church."

He again pointed skyward. "I never trained Shiloh to do that. It's simply divine intervention."

Alas, I never found any doughnut holes that morning.

CHAPTER 50
Homework Angels

If you can't learn from a Dog, you can't learn.

—Shiloh

I have met a lot of Barb's and Barbara's in my life.
Minister Randy's assistant is one of them. Even though
she's married, everyone calls her Miss Barbara. Her path
to the ministry was very unusual and impressive. After
thirty years as a nurse and devout church member, she made
a right turn and switched careers to help the Lord. Part of
her job at the church was being in charge of the Homework
Angels program.

The term *angel* describes both the students and their
volunteer teachers. On Tuesdays at 4:00 p.m., children
arrive at three rooms located in the back of the church
building, where they receive tutoring on the subjects in
which they are having trouble. The children, from the

first grade through the fifth grade, come from a nearby elementary school, and most of them are Guatemalan.

Jerry and I had heard the phrase, "Homework Angels," mentioned at church service. I assumed that the word *angels* meant that it was a special church group.

One day after church, Miss Barbara asked Jerry if he was good in math. Jerry responded, "Probably my best subject. Why?"

Miss Barbara smiled. Jerry was about to become an angel without even leaving the earth. She suggested that I not come because some of the young children might be frightened by me. Several of the kids had come from difficult circumstances, where Dogs were used mostly to guard homes.

Jerry was the only male angel, which is consistent with the Bible. He was having little success with two fifth graders, who were goofing off and had no interest in working on their homework. His usual creative ideas didn't seem to work.

Then he went to Miss Barbara with a plan. He took me to the thirty-minute recess that followed the 4:00 to 5:00 p.m. homework session. I stayed outside and only the children who had completed their homework and weren't afraid of me or allergic to Dogs came outside to play with me. They were cute kids. They threw a ball and chased me around the church lawn. After a while, Miss Barbara and the other ladies brought out the refreshments. Jesús and Juan, the two troublemakers, tried to crash the party but Jerry disciplined them through tough love. He told the boys that they knew the rules and they didn't qualify to be out there because they hadn't finished their homework. They accused Jerry of being unfair, and he told them that if they really wanted to be involved in the outdoor fun and refreshment, it was easy to qualify.

"Look around. All the other kids did it and they are younger than the two of you," Jerry said.

The toughies then used some swear words in Spanish. Jerry responded, "I speak Spanish, so be careful boys."

After a few sessions went the same way, Jerry got permission from Miss Barbara to let me come inside during the tutoring. It turned out that I had won over the few children who thought they might be afraid. My calmness and gentleness had come through again.

Jerry's next plan was to split the two troublemakers into different rooms. He finally broke through each of their defenses by giving them the incentive of playing ball with me, taking me for a walk, and having me do some tricks for them after they had completed their homework. As I laid under the table, I heard Jerry using me as an example in his math problems, comparing and computing Dog years and human years. He used me as an example in all forms of math, until they came to fractions. I was unwilling to be only a portion of myself. My master used a different example and I felt at ease once again.

By the end of the school year, the two troublemakers had learned a lot from Jerry and me about math, as well as other lessons.

My master and I also worked together to show and explain how to properly treat and care for a Dog. Several of the children learned as much here as they had in their homework studies.

We were both very proud of Jesús and Juan. Together, the four of us learned a lot at Homework Angels.

CHAPTER 51

Boys of Greensboro

A Dog is boy's best friend.

—Shiloh

J erry's youngest grandchildren, Jared and Charlie, moved to Greensboro, North Carolina, in 2007 with their parents, Chris and Kathy. This made me sad because they have a great Dog named Chloe who might be even faster than Dekeon was. Whenever they came to Jerry and Barb's, Chloe and I would race down the stairs to the lake and sprint up and down the beach. The only odd thing about Chloe was that she refused to go near the water. Whoever heard of a Dog that didn't like water, other than Missy?

Chloe was great at retrieving tennis balls, and we'd have contests to see who could reach a ball first. But I knew that I'd be the winner whenever the ball went in or near the water. Maybe that's why she moved to Greensboro, which is a beautiful place with very few lakes.

As part of our routine, we now stop in Greensboro on the way down to Florida for the winter or on our way back to Michigan. After twelve hours in the car, I am ready to run, and as soon as my master opens the door I leap out. Within seconds Chloe is nipping at my heels as we race around her yard.

For some reason Jerry is always yelling at me to slow down. I guess he thinks that I'm getting old, but if anybody should know that you don't have to let age slow you down, it's him.

Chloe has a big back yard in the woods, and I can always find something good to play with, like a pile of leaves, or if I'm lucky, a dead chipmunk. I know that humans don't understand, but there is nothing better than getting some good animal stink on you. It makes other Dogs respect you more.

I'll be heading to Chloe's pretty soon, so I hope that she's been hiding some old tennis balls around the yard. I'm ready to play!

On December 25, 2010, Greensboro received its first snow on Christmas Day since 1947. Six inches of the fluffy, white stuff fell to the ground to the delight of many people.

I had to reacquaint Chloe about how to roll in it and make dog snow angels. The temperature was nineteen degrees and because she has short hair, she kept running back into the house.

I stayed out for most of the day, watching Chris and my master help Jared and Charlie build a large snowman. A few days later we said our goodbyes and as we drove out of the driveway, I detected a bit of a tear in the snowman's left eye. I'm glad we left before the majestic snowman thawed and turned to mush.

CHAPTER 52

Sara's School Revisited

I tell you the truth, unless you change and become
like little children, you will never enter the kingdom
of Heaven.

—Jesus of Nazareth

We returned to Michigan and visit Glenn Elementary School for the annual wrap-up of the school year. Glenn Elementary is the oldest continuously operated elementary school in Michigan. It dates back to 1854. Until just a few years ago, it was a one-room schoolhouse. These days, more families are leaving the big city life of Chicago and moving to the shores of Lake Michigan, where they find fabulous fruit farms, water-oriented activities, wonderful forest opportunities, and the benefits of small town rural life. This returning to nature has resulted in Glenn Elementary School's expansion.

Great teachers have always been attracted to this historic little school. Now some big-city children are receiving a great education and experiencing a simpler lifestyle. I've found that these children often don't relate well to animals simply because they haven't been around them as much. I take it on myself to be a great role model for all of my animal brethren.

You may recall me saying that my master and I have our Dog and pony show down to a science. This year, however, we were in for some surprises.

After holding our usual question and answer session about how Dogs help humans, we heard the most creative story yet. Timmy, who is eight years old, told us that his Dog, Einstein, knew over five hundred words and could hum one hundred songs. I was surprised but relieved that Timmy didn't claim that Einstein had written his own book.

When we thought we were done, Sara, the little girl who had previously asked for my autograph, asked for my autograph once again. Jerry dropped to his knees and prepared to help me sign my paw print when suddenly Sara presented me with a burlap tote bag and a permanent marker. The children had made these tote bags as their project for the end of the school year. Jerry wrote, "To Sara. Have a super safe sunny summer. Love, Shiloh."

I could see that my master was pleased with himself, but he didn't see what I saw: twenty-three kids in line with all of their tote bags. Now, some serious signing was required. As the kid's bags were completed, they began to compare Jerry's comments. Thereafter, he had to write twenty-three different messages.

When Jerry was finished, the teacher had to help him get to his feet. He looked around for our nemesis, Sara, but she was long gone.

And so another adventure with the Glenn school children ended. I never get bored around those kids. They always come up with new and fresh ideas.

CHAPTER 53

Surprise Birthday with Lindsay

L.O.L. = Laughing Out Loud

—Webster's New Dictionary

Every May after we return from Florida to the lake house, Jerry calls his granddaughter, Lindsay, in Traverse City to announce that we'll be at her birthday party on the fourth of June. Her comment is always the same: "Grandma and Grandpa, yes. Shiloh, no."

I think it's cool that we share the same birthday and I've always liked Lindsay a lot. She's doggone cool. She loves her Dog, Missy, but she too is excluded from the festivities. It's probably just a teenage girl thing. Since I love girls I reluctantly accept her yearly decision to exclude me.

One year Jerry had that impish smile that told me when something goofy and fun was on the horizon. I jumped into the Suburban with Jerry and Barb and drove to Traverse City. We pulled up on the street side of the Red

Ginger Restaurant and Barb went inside. Traverse City is consistently voted one of the Best Small Towns in America to live. The only downside is that one cannot find a place to park on the main street downtown. We drove around behind the restaurant and found a place in an alley by the back door. Their door was locked, so we entered the back entrance of the bookstore next door. As we approached the front of the Horizon Books store, we saw that there was a lot of commotion. A thirteen-year-old author was having a book signing for her first publication. I thought that it was absolutely amazing that an author could be that young, and then I realized that I was even younger and I am writing a book too. The young girl was quite extraordinary, and when Jerry bought a copy of her book, I offered her my left paw, which she happily accepted, as my way of congratulating her. Jerry told me that it's a sign of good luck for me to shake people's hands with my left paw.

We left the bookstore and walked next door to the Red Ginger Restaurant. Barb and Addie, Lindsay's other grandma, were seated at a table with five chairs along the wall. There were also eight chairs at a table in the middle of the room. I knew that it would be time for Lindsay to appear soon. Humans don't think I can read time, but I saw that it was 6:00 p.m. At 6:15 p.m., six of Lindsay's teenage girlfriends arrived with presents and balloons. They said their hellos and then began decorating the birthday party table. While we were waiting, Steve, the manager, came over to talk with us, and he commented on how nicely the young ladies were decorating his restaurant. He had seen me when I arrived and asked Jerry many questions about my therapy work. Because he obviously loved Dogs, I thought that he was special enough to mention him in my book. Jerry indicated with his hand for me to go under the special table and await Lindsay's arrival.

At 6:30 p.m. they came: Mark, Anne, and her sister Carly, who had picked up Lindsay at her Mom's store Cherry Hill Boutique, which was a block away. Lindsay had closed the store for her Mom and was telling her of a last big sale when all of a sudden the table in the middle of the room erupted and everyone was hugging and laughing and singing, "Happy Birthday!" Then she saw her grandparents table and went over there to hug and kiss them and tell them what a great surprise their presence was.

"I'm shocked you didn't smuggle Shiloh in on our Birthday," she said to her grandpa.

Jerry responded, "Wow that would have been great. Two birthdays together."

Five minutes later, when Lindsay was settled at her table, I moved to her side from my hiding place, and put my nose on her lap.

This was her second big surprise of the day, and she leaped out of her chair. After regaining her composure, she exclaimed, "Grandpa!"

Yeah, I finally got to share my birthday with Lindsay and vice-versa.

CHAPTER 54

On the Radio

The more I see of man,
The more I like Dogs.

—Mme. de Stael

I always thought that television would be the best medium for me to tell my amazing story, partly because I am nice to look at, and I have a certain presence that can be entertaining. All kidding aside, I was delighted when I was invited to be on a radio show and Jerry accepted the invitation on my behalf.

It was a Saturday morning live broadcast from the Coral Gables Annex in Saugatuck. Jerry couldn't resist the lure of free doughnuts and coffee. We arrived early. Jerry had coffee and sinkers and I, as usual, had nothing.

I'd heard his phrase a hundred times: "Oh, nothing for Shiloh. He doesn't eat human food." "Oh yeah," I always thought to myself. I'd eat it all if someone offered it. I do admit that at home I get to lick and thereby pre-wash the dishes in the dishwashing machine before they close the door. All the yummy food crumbs and stains disappear under my efficient tongue. My favorite dishwashing duty is to remove the runny egg tracks off of the breakfast dishes. That's ambrosia for me. I'm not sure why Barb feels it's necessary to wash these dishes after I've done such a good job.

The radio show co-hosts were rambling on with another guest and I was concerned that he was infringing on my time. He was some local government official who seemed very impressed with himself. I'm not being unkind. This was just the way it appeared to me. Meanwhile, the wives of the co-hosts were taking turns petting me. I love this, especially if it's two attractive, smelling like fresh powder and lemon, human females. While my master went to refill his coffee, one of the women slipped me a bit of brioche, which was very continental.

The co-hosts kept yakking away until I finally heard my introduction: "Next, we have the Star of Saugatuck." I immediately got up, but was upstaged by the owner of the excursion boat, The Star of Saugatuck. I went back under the table, hoping to get some more continental crumbs, but soon I fell asleep. At this rate, I'll never get on television, I thought.

I was aware of my master moving to sit with the co-hosts. "This is Jerry Hill who has a very special Therapy Dog named Showno." "Whoa," I thought. "It's Shiloh, and I'm not a no-show. I'm right here." But the morning radio jockeys were asking Jerry all about himself. I should have brought Timmy's Dog, Einstein, from Glenn Elementary

School to speak up for me. He could use his vast five-hundred-word vocabulary.

The broadcast was over and the talking heads finally wanted to meet me. They offered me their right hands and I offered them my left paw. I wasn't in sync with these guys, who obviously had no interest in my future TV career. I've heard it said and now I know it's true: Radio is dead.

CHAPTER 55

Stairs to the Big Lake

To sit with a Dog on a hillside on a glorious afternoon,
Is to be back in Eden where doing nothing was not boring—
It was peace.

—Milan Kundera

At least once every day when we are in Michigan Jerry will say, "Shiloh, let's go to the Big Lake." We live on a bluff that looks straight west, somewhere between Chicago and Milwaukee, on one of the largest fresh water lakes in the world, Lake Michigan.

We headed down the sixty-one steps to the beach and walked south for a half mile. I loved this walk. I ran through dune grasses sniffing new miscellaneous items that had washed up on shore, like driftwood or deflated balloons that have traveled the ninety miles across the lake from Wisconsin. Occasionally I came upon a great foul-smelling dead fish. After the extensive training Sherry gave me early in my life, Jerry would use her technique of saying "No, Shiloh" to keep me away from fish, porcupines, and skunks. I have regressed a bit in this training at times, but now, in my now senior status, I avoid all of the above obstacles like the plague.

When there were no waves, I would always wade in for a quick swim. Big waves spook me. I only swim in calm waters. Fearful of the rip tide that sometimes accompanies big waves, I imagine I could be carried all the way out to Milwaukee. I think my Dog paddling prowess would only take me a short way in the lake. Wisely, I stayed near shore.

When we reached the end of our half-mile walk down the beach, we turned east, up through the cut, as Jerry calls it. The cut is a small gorge that goes really high up. It is the equivalent of the sixty-one stair steps to the top of the bluff. We are now on Wau-Ke-Na property, a nature conservancy. In the Potawatomi language, Wau-Ke-Na means "Forest by the water."

On this day in September, Jerry stopped abruptly and held out his hand to tell me to stop and stay. I obeyed. We both gazed into the eyes of the biggest and most beautiful whitetail buck that I have ever seen. This twelve-point deer still had some velvet hanging from his antlers. (Velvet is the furry-like protection that appears every year when a buck's antlers grow. As fall approaches the buck rubs his antlers on small trees to remove the velvet and prepares himself for the rut-mating season.) It seemed like an eternity, but in Dog-time it was only a matter of a few seconds before the great buck ran away looking absolutely majestic. It was only then I noticed a beautiful doe running off behind him.

Jerry turned and released me from my "sit, stay" command by saying "Good boy, Shiloh," but I heard a bit of a tremor in his voice. We went to the bench at the edge of the bluff that looks toward the great lake, and Jerry sat down like he always does on our walks. I normally wander around and roll in the grass, but for some reason, perhaps because I was also greatly affected by the sight of the great buck and the doe, I laid down at my master's feet. I'm not sure whether he was talking to me or to himself. Here's what he had to say:

"Shiloh, I don't know about you, but something transformed me when I looked into that buck's eyes. Although I've been a deer hunter all my life, I am choosing now to never shoot another deer. I'll still go to deer camp with my sons and friends. I'll still do the cooking and we'll still ride on the property and observe the beautiful creatures, but Shiloh, this is personal. It has nothing to do with anyone else's hunting philosophy. It's just mine."

And Jerry has never killed another deer.

I was also awed by the grandeur of the buck and the doe. It seemed in the natural order of things for those two to have their forest to run in and not have to worry about being shot.

Jerry often prayed on the bench we were sitting on. He spoke the Lord's Prayer aloud, followed by special prayers for all of his family members and the leaders of our country to make the right decisions. He said a special personal prayer for me, and I love him for that.

I also pray every time that Jerry prays. It's a silent prayer, but I want to share it with you: "Lord, help me to be as good a Dog as my Master thinks I am."

After our prayers, we head home across the bluff and up the dirt road that leads to our house. I must divulge a little secret that some Dog trainers wouldn't endorse. Jerry carries small Dog biscuits in his pocket on these walks. I know the command, "Stay with me," which means I'm supposed to stay within a certain radius and look back to my master regularly for direction. I continually come back to him during the walk for those wonderful Dog treats. When we periodically go to a pet store, they have four sizes of Dog biscuits: large, medium, small and puppies! Unfortunately, he always buys the puppy size. He makes sure that they are good for my teeth and breath. They are also very good for my morale.

So goes the life of a blessed Therapy Dog!

CHAPTER 56

SOTE

Salt of the Earth
—Matthew 5:13

When we began writing my book, twice a week Jerry and I would go to a lovely restaurant in Fennville, Michigan, called Salt of the Earth to wait for my ghostwriter, Colleen. She began as a ghostwriter but eventually she and Jerry decided to co-author my memoir. This was perfectly all right with me, although they never asked my opinion.

When we arrived at the restaurant, Lisa, the woman behind the counter, would exclaim, "Here comes Shiloh…" People always recognize me and sometimes they recognize Jerry too. Jerry got coffee and took me to a table. Colleen arrived, sat down, and the chatter began. They talked about me and told stories of emotion, joy and adventure, yet neither Colleen nor Jerry ever addressed or even looked at me. Oh, I take that back. Colleen patted me on the head, shook my paw, and then went back to talking to Jerry. Back when Colleen was referred to as the ghostwriter, I didn't think she was spooky. In fact, I thought she was really nice and smelled like fields of lavender.

Another place that I love to go is the post office. Every day but Sunday we visit the Glenn, Michigan Post Office. If there's a line, I fall in at the end and wait my turn to put my paws up on the counter, where Diane or Jackie says to me, "Hi Shiloh," and gives me a Dog biscuit. On occasion, I will go directly to the head of the line and I've received my reward more quickly. Then Jerry will scold me good-naturedly and everyone will laugh. I do this when he is getting all of our mail from the PO box. I say, "all of *our* mail," but in reality it's all for Barb and Jerry.

After visiting the post office, we headed back to the Salt of the Earth, where Jerry read his mail and the USA Today newspaper. He had more coffee and I had more time to spend on the floor. If I'm lucky, there are a few delectable crumbs from a cookie or a biscotti under the table just waiting for me to clean them up.

We said goodbye to Lisa and went to the Golden Orchards Lifehouse, a nearby Christian retirement facility. In the lobby of Golden Orchards there was a fox that just stared at me. I steered clear of it and made a wide berth. While a staff member suggested whom to visit on that day, Jerry related my concerns about the stuffed fox. The staff member just laughed, but I've always wondered about what the fox was stuffed with. I contemplated taking a quick bite out of him to see what he's made of, but my better judgment fortunately took over, and I left so that he could scare the next Dog or puppy that entered the building.

We made a few therapy visits and then went back to the house on Lake Michigan where Jerry and Barb live. Having served a good deed for the day, I decided that it was time for a nap.

I awake to good news. Jerry and Barb were talking about going to Salt of the Earth for dinner. That night the restaurant was busy and noisy. I fell asleep until a delicious morsel dropped within inches of my nose. It smelled so good and I wolfed it down in a microsecond. I've always enjoyed my evening floor time at Salt of the Earth because I receive more morsels of food fall on the floor at night than in the morning.

CHAPTER 57

Camp Hope

Love is giving for the world's needs,
love is sharing as the Spirit leads,
love is caring when the world cries,
love is compassion with Christ-like eyes.

—Brandt

Camp Hope is very special therapy opportunity that comes in August of every year at the Hospice of Holland. It is a bereavement camp for CHILDREN who have experienced the death of a close relative.

I believe that the greatest benefit of Camp Hope is that CHILDREN come to understand that they are not alone in this world. They come to the realization that other CHILDREN have lost loved ones and they too are grieving. They talk openly about their own experiences. I'm always saddened by the despair that they verbalize, and in times like this I always wish that I had the ability to talk like a human so that I could give the CHILDREN more comfort. I'm thankful that I've been blessed with the ability to communicate my thoughts to my master so that he can put them in print.

At Camp Hope I made myself available for the kids to hug and pet me, while the CHILDREN provided their own therapy by sharing their experiences of grief with each other. I felt somewhat inadequate at this time so I looked forward to the balloon release.

One activity that helped the CHILDREN with their grief involved them writing a note to their deceased loved one, attaching it to a balloon, and releasing the balloons together. I loved seeing the expressions on their faces as they watched the balloons rise into the sky. The activity helped them bear witness to the love and connection that they had experienced with their loved one, and it provided them a shared experience of the loss and healing that binds everyone together.

The people who work at hospices are for the most part volunteers. Many have experienced the loss of their own loved ones. They understand what the CHILDREN are going through, and they are able to empathize with them. Nothing is more poignant than watching a CHILD cry in grief for the parent they have lost. If I had arms, I would want to gather them up in my arms and hold them tightly to comfort them. Instead, I go to them and nose them and they usually end up hugging me tightly around my neck. If they squeeze a little I don't mind. I know I am giving them comfort and unconditional love.

This wonderful place is called Camp Hope but I call it Camp Love. The Hospice of Holland's core purpose is to support not only patients but also families facing illness and grief. Camp Hope- Love certainly fulfills this mission.

CHAPTER 58

What I've learned as a Therapy Dog

Be not afraid of going slowly;
be afraid only of standing still.

—Chinese Proverb

As Samuel Johnson said, "Self-confidence is the first requisite to great therapy work."

Here are some things I've learned to do as a Therapy Dog: Make eye contact with the humans. Be careful not to smile with your teeth because it scares many humans, especially children.

Whenever humans look at you, wag your tail continuously.

When humans talk about you for more than sixty seconds, lie down and take a short nap, especially if you're over ten years old.

Every time you get up off the floor, stretch to rid your body of tension and stress.

Be Positive. Don't let the chipmunks and squirrels get you down. Never chase anything you don't want to catch or anything you know you can't outrun.

As Confucius says, "Wherever you go, go with all your heart."

Humans will provide you with water and food for nourishment. However, you must find your own inspiration to be a successful Therapy Dog.

In her book, *Through a Dog's Eyes*, Jennifer Arnold provides a scientific argument for what Dog lovers everywhere already know: Dogs love, trust, sense, and feel, and they deserve to be treated accordingly. Jennifer Arnold emphasizes using only choice-based positive reinforcement training methods, and I was fortunate enough to have been trained for therapy work in that manner.

Some tips to becoming a successful Therapy Dog include having a passion to serve, a big loving heart, excellent conditioning, and a high-quality diet.

It helps to be born a golden retriever because we're all about service. We are loyal and very gentle with everyone, especially children.

You must grow in your ability to comfort those people who will soon make their final transitions, and you must accept death.

One key to being a successful therapy Dog is to do absolutely nothing on your days off and not feel guilty about it.

It helps to be fortunate enough to have a sensitive and kind master.

Teamwork with your master divides the effort and multiplies the effect.

Over the years we've spent together, my master and I have learned a lot from each other.

Helen Keller said, "The best and most beautiful things in the world cannot be seen or touched but are felt in the heart."

Finally, reflect upon experiences that have touched you deeply and record those feelings in a book like I have done in *Shiloh Speaks*.

CHAPTER 59

Besides Therapy Work I Make

BFF = Best Friends Forever

—Shiloh and Jerry

In addition to being a Therapy Dog, here is a list of some things I function as:

A good pillow

A good dress-up model for the holidays (Sometimes Jerry's granddaughters put hats and decorations on me. I am always very good about accepting whatever they dress me in.)

A good newspaper delivery Dog

A good therapist

A good girl magnet

A good hugger

A good licker

A good confidante

A good friend, forever

A good dishwasher
A good conversation piece
A good animal-spotter in the forest
A compassionate bed-side companion
Last, but not least, a good story teller

CHAPTER 60

Get Lucky

Live a good life. In the end, it's not the years in a life, it's the life in the years.

—Abraham Lincoln

I am lucky to be born in the USA.

I am lucky to have an owner who loves me, plays with me every day, and takes me for long walks, preferably off a leash so that I can roam and explore this wonderful world that Dogs and humans share.

Be able to roam in the north woods.

Have a master like Jerry, who brags that he and Sherry trained me, but doesn't realize that I've also trained him. Spend some time alone every day.

Have an owner who allows me to grow my gentle, trusting nature, and who has insights into Dog-human interaction and sincerely believes that my therapy work is an important contribution to humankind.

Everywhere we go people remark about how lucky I am to have a master like Jerry and how lucky Jerry is to have a Dog like me. Also, Barb tells stories about how lucky her husband is and their three sons do likewise. On the golf course it's the same. People on the golf course often say "Lucky shot," and during card games they say, "You're so lucky!" Here's my question: Are we born lucky or is there some mystical force that controls events in this world? My master has told me that people have been asking this question since the beginning of time. Does something outside of us control events? When I go to church with my master I hear the minister talk about this very concept. I have no clue to the answers of these universal questions, but I am convinced that my master and I are among the lucky ones. Neither luck nor happiness is a destination, but rather they are part of a day-by-day journey.

I am lucky to be able to provide comfort to the life-threatened and sick, as well as CHILDREN who are grieving for their lost loved one.

It helps to have other Dogs as friends and companions.

It's nice to have a supportive and loving family and extended family like Jerry's grandchildren, sons, and daughters-in-law.

Count your many blessings and you'll see how incredibly lucky you're been. You have so many blessings that you'll soon lose count.

CHAPTER 61

Saddle Bags and the Ramp

Growing old isn't for sissies.

—Shiloh

About a year ago, one of my buddies, a Bernese mountain Dog named Kally, passed away at the young age of seven. Her master, John, gave us her unused Dog food and a ramp that Kally had used in her last year. The ramp folded up and fit nicely in the back of a SUV. When opened, it was twice its original size, and it functioned as a walkway into the Suburban.

Jerry told John, we'll take the food and give it to the Humane Society, but we don't need the ramp. On hearing this, I nudged him and he immediately got my ESP signal.

"John, we'll take the ramp, after all," he then said. He stored it in the garage in a place where we would completely forget about it.

A few months later I didn't make it when I attempted to jump into the Suburban. The truck is quite high and all of a sudden I couldn't leap gracefully like I normally could. I was quite surprised, but after a few weeks of aborted jumping efforts, my master said, "Shiloh, the time has come. You're twelve years old."

I found these words alarming, as I had lost a few buddies over the past year. However, he rummaged through the garage until he found Kally's old ramp. He extended it, placed one end at the floor level in the truck and the other on the ground.

"Up, Shy," he said.

I climbed halfway up and jumped off. The ramp seemed too high and foreign to me.

After considerable coaxing, Jerry said sternly, "Shiloh, up."

I walked up the ramp, and while my master went to get something from the house, I walked back down the ramp and lay down in the driveway pretending to be asleep.

When he came out of the house and found me on the driveway, he didn't seem amused as he said to me, "Into the truck, Shiloh. Up."

Up I went again and he immediately folded the ramp and slid it next to me, closing the rear gate.

Whenever I use the ramp to re-enter the truck, we always seem to attract a crowd of onlookers. Jerry's set comment is, "A few more years and I'll probably use it too." This always evokes a few laughs, but I don't find it funny.

A year earlier, when I was eleven years old, I had started growing sack-like bags on my sides. My vet examined them, took some samples, and diagnosed them as fatty, non-cancerous tumors, known medically as Lipoma.

We were both relieved at the diagnosis, and we have them re-checked every three months.

When Barb and Jerry's grandsons saw them, they named them Shiloh's Saddle Bags.

As I grow older, I must be losing my sense of humor because I don't see the humor in this.

CHAPTER 62

Dreamgirls

A woman is like an artichoke
you must work hard to get to her heart.

—Inspector Jacques Clouseau, The Pink Panther

I t was getting cold and wintery, so we packed to head
back to Stuart, Florida. Jerry was pretty clever. On the
basement floor he laid out the dimensions of the interior
bed of the Suburban truck. He had three categories of stuff
to be packed: S (Shiloh) = highest priority for my food, bed,
toys, etc. B (Barb) = second highest priority for all of her
clothes. J (Jerry) = lowest priority for golf clubs, golf shoes,
and any room that's left for only his most essential stuff.

It didn't look like everything would make the trip, but
somehow it all fit and so we went on our way. I spent most
of the time sleeping in my designated space and on my
comfy bed, dreaming away the miles.

I confess that most of my dreams are about females, both humans and canines. It's always my best sense that dictates my choice. If they smell good I like them. Jerry likes girls, which Barb says is harmless, and his selection seems to be based on looks. In addition, we're both attracted to the smarter sex when they're especially nice to Dogs. Since we are both attracted to the same girls, does that mean that I'm more like a human or Jerry is more like a Dog?

There are a lot of wonderful girls in Michigan, including our next-door neighbor Alice and Missy, the dog from Traverse City that I mentioned in chapter 46. However, using the discipline of conservation, I'm going to focus more on the GIRLS of Florida.

As soon as we arrived in the Sunshine State, my master and I headed to the ocean and walked along the beach on our way to the Tiki Bar and Grill.

"Shazam!" I thought to myself. All of my favorites were working that day: Cheryl, Regina, and Bridget. They gave lots of hugs to both of us. A dish of cold water arrived while we were getting caught up on what had happened in the past seven months since we left.

Our next stop was the Ocean Club Golf Shop, where one of my favorite people, Janet, was working. She gave us more hugs and updated us about her cat, Mandy. Then, as a bonus, Ginny arrived for her shift. We talked with her about more of the same stuff, then I headed to the condo feeling like the most loved and hugged Dog in Florida.

The next day we ran errands and stopped in to see Cecilia, our talented and beautiful Pilates instructor, and all of the women of the Treasure Coast Hospice Volunteer office. I received hugs and Dog treats from Eileen and Kathy and thought, "It's great to be back!"

Tonight's sleep will be filled with thoughts about my favorite Florida dream girls.

CHAPTER 63

The Bell Ringer

*There is no reward equal to that of doing
the most good to the most people in the most need
without discrimination.*

—Evangeline Booth

Shortly after arriving back in Florida, we received our schedule for being bell ringers for the Salvation Army. I had been a volunteer bell ringer for several years in Michigan, and we were in Florida for the Holiday season. We were assigned to be outside of a Super Walmart on Friday and Saturday evenings from 6:00 to 8:00 p.m.

On some nights R. T. and Mary Brown, two other volunteers, helped us out. Barb was there also, and everyone but me wore the Salvation Army's red apron.

Approximately one thousand people entered and exited the store in each two-hour period. Our goal was to invite everyone to place money in the red kettle. I sat next to the kettle, which was perfect for people to pet me or have their picture taken with me. Either way it usually resulted in a contribution.

We saw several Spanish-speaking families, and the kids would ask their parents about the beautiful Dog. I prefer to be called handsome, but I'll take anything for a donation. My master would invite them in Spanish to come closer because I was very friendly. R. T. led our team by chanting and singing. He was a terrible singer, but he was effective at slowing people down long enough to get their contribution.

I think I'm a pretty good judge of people, but I was continually amazed at the well-dressed folks who gave us nothing and the poorly dressed families who gave generously. Many young kids would pet me, shake my paw, talk to their parents, and return with a few coins. I have learned some wonderful lessons from observing people's generosity.

Most nights were very warm and we were all exhausted from hawking and soliciting donations to help the Salvation Army do its good work.

Another volunteer, Charlie, arrived to relieve us at 8:00 p.m., and we headed toward our vehicle. Without needing the ramp, I jumped in, grateful for my master, his family, and the friends who have shaped my life. I felt thankful for the special moments of service that I'd been privileged to give to people. Peace enveloped me and I fell immediately into a deep sleep.

CHAPTER 64

Indiantown

Throughout its lifetime an elephant goes through six sets of teeth. The elephant starves to death once the sixth set of teeth falls out.

—Facts by Jack

One Sunday morning a lady from church petted me on the head and said, "Shiloh, would you come to the school at Indiantown to visit the fourth graders? They are reading a book called Shiloh and I know that they would love to meet you." My master looked at me and I knew he would accept the offer.

Twenty miles west of Stuart, Indiantown is a very poor area. Jerry had certain expectations about our visit, but he turned out to be very wrong. We arrived at a run-down building, which was the home of the Hope Rural School.

Before we entered, our friend from church greeted us warmly. Once inside, we were welcomed with applause.

We looked at the smiling, well-scrubbed faces in their neatly pressed green shirts, and we were blown away. These were the brightest and most optimistic kids we had ever encountered.

After we were introduced, my master said, "I bet we all have something in common."

A young man raised his hand and asked politely, "What would that be, Mr. Hill?"

Jerry answered, "I was a bus student just like you."

Another student asked, "What was the name of your school?"

Again Jerry answered, "W. K. Kellogg Consolidated Agricultural School of Hickory Corners, Michigan."

The teacher looked amazed. "You can't be serious?"

"Yes. We used to kid that if you could say the name of the school, you would graduate."

"Mr. Hill, I too graduated from Kellogg!"

My master and the teacher immediately bonded and we had the best experience ever at an elementary school.

The fifth grade had joined the fourth grade, so it was a bigger group than normal. However, they were great kids with good manners.

A fifth-grade girl raised her hand and asked, "Do you brush Shiloh's teeth?"

"I sure do. I brought his toothbrush and toothpaste with us. Do I have a volunteer?"

The children were tickled at this and they giggled.

The same girl quickly raised her hand, "I'll do it!"

As everyone watched, many of them in disbelief, Yami brushed my teeth with my master's help. She was special in my book because she let me lick the excess off the toothbrush. It was a chicken flavor, my favorite.

After a question and answer session we headed outside for recess, where I retrieved tennis balls and ran some figure eights around the schoolyard. The teacher called everyone together to thank us with another round of applause.

Jerry told the two classes that they were the most attentive and neatly dressed and that they gave the most smiles of any group we had ever met. He continued telling them how proud we were of all of them and their teacher. He told them that we'd be back next year and told them that "Shiloh expects that all of you have been brushing your teeth and caring for your pets."

CHAPTER 65

Snowbirds

Birds of a feather
flock together.

—Unknown

In the local paper, a reporter we'll call Ed made a statement that the snowbirds had returned, which meant that there would be longer lines at the super market and more traffic congestion. He finished by saying, "What positive contribution do snowbirds make to our community?"

One evening several offended snowbirds were gathered as a flock at our little condo for food and beverages. Before I knew it, Jerry had accepted their challenge to take on the reporter's accusations. He would spend a day with the correspondent so that he could observe a snowbird's contribution to the area.

It started at 9:00 a.m., when we picked up the reporter for his day of adventure. Our first stop was a golf shop, where I carried my leash in my mouth and we visited all of the employees. Jerry bought some golf equipment and the reporter recorded this on his camcorder. Next we went to the Pilates studio, where Cecilia gave me a hug and talked about upcoming sessions with Barb and Jerry.

Across the street to the Goodwill Industries drive-through, my master donated some unused clothing. After that we stopped by the pet store to buy two big bags of my special food.

Since it was a Tuesday, we went to the shoe store because they were having a sale where you buy one pair of tennis shoes at full price and get the second pair at half price. In addition, they took 10 percent off of the entire transaction because Jerry is a veteran.

"I was in the marines, but I knew nothing of that Tuesday deal," Ed said.

Stay with us, kid. We'll educate you, I said to myself.

After that, we visited a hospital and then a hospice, where the reporter was asked to put away his camcorder and wait for us in the lobby.

We visited three life-threatened people and then returned to our astonished reporter.

We went through the drive-in at a local pharmacy to pick up Barb's special medicine, which cost over one thousand dollars for a one-month supply. Jerry showed the sales slip to the reporter so that he would realize how much a snowbird spends in his town.

Jerry picked up some cleaning and then visited Nina, a one-hundred-year-old lady from our church. As the three of us walked down hallways of the rehab facility to Nina's room, several staff members stopped to pet me and shake my paw. They frequently greeted me by saying, "Hey, Shiloh. How you been?"

I smiled at them, as if to say, "I've been fine. Thanks."

After our visit with Nina, we stopped at our golf course, where Joe the Pro told the reporter that 90 percent of his members were snowbirds. Ed was flabbergasted at this high number. We were really educating him.

Then it was time for lunch. We stopped at our condo, where Ed met Barb. Instead of going on a thirty-minute beach walk with me, Ed talked with Barb about the money we spend annually on maintenance fees, property taxes, and insurance, as well as our many restaurant, super market and movie expenses.

I needed to pee, so my master took me for a walk after arranging to meet Barb and Ed at the Tiki for lunch. We had a good time and some good conversation, and the three of us agreed later that Ed was a good man. We were, however, anxious to see what he wrote about his day with two snowbirds.

True to his word, Ed wrote nothing but nice things about snowbirds, especially about the two who let him follow them around for a day on their many trips of volunteering and shopping. He realized that these two snowbirds brought many benefits to the people of Stuart.

My master and I were proud to represent the many snowbirds that are vital to the economy of this Florida community.

CHAPTER 66

The Talking Dog

Dogs talk. They talk to each other,
they talk to you.

—Shiloh

Now that you've read my book this far, you might be thinking that even though I'm speaking to you in this book, no Dog can really talk. It's time to tell you one of my favorite Dog stories.

Charlie the collie was considered by his family to be the Black Sheep of the litter. He was eventually banished to life on a farm far from the city life he had grown to love.

One day the farmer at his new home had enough, and put a sign in the yard that said: "Talking Collie Dog for sale—$10."

A passerby stopped his car and inquired about the ten-dollar Dog.

"I love Collies and I'm interested in one that can talk," he said.

"He talks all right," the farmer said. "You can't shut him up. He's in the back bedroom. Go take a look and if he's watching the Playboy channel, turn off the TV."

The man went into the bedroom and asked, "You're the talking Dog?"

"Yep," said the Dog.

"What are you watching on TV.?"

"The Westminster Dog Show, but Collies never win!"

"The man was utterly amazed and began asking questions.

"What's your name?"

"Charlie," the dog said. Charlie answered all the man's questions. He told him that he discovered his unusual talent when he was just a puppy. He had been on the road with a rock band for a year, and then he went into the CIA. After that he grew bored and became a bomb sniffer Dog and eventually graduated to working as a Rescue Dog in the Alaskan Wilderness. A tour with the Army in Iraq further sharpened his bomb skills, and after becoming injured and receiving a Purple Heart, he retired. But when the Transportation Security Authority, or TSA, needed help with identifying terrorists, he returned to active duty until he over-sniffed a female passenger and was placed on leave, without pay. This was his present situation and he was contemplating writing a book about his life.

I'm thinking, "Let's hope not. That would be too much competition.

The man who had stopped on a lark was flabbergasted, so he returned to see the farmer and told him, "Your Dog just told me his life story, and what a fantastic story it was! How can you sell this amazing Dog for only ten dollars?"

"Because he tells fibs and exaggerates the truth."

CHAPTER 67

The Big C

Get regular check-ups.

—Shiloh and Jerry

Busy as usual, we had been back in Florida for a few weeks when Barb and Jerry had one of those serious talks. Barb was the realist and Jerry was the dreamer. Barb took the lead and reminded him that he had been very tired over the past several months. The last time he had his blood work done it looked suspicious and he had promised his Michigan doctor that he would have additional blood tests. In addition, he was due for a colonoscopy. Thinking that he was bulletproof, Jerry protested but Barb won.

The blood tests confirmed the Michigan doctors concerns. The colonoscopy was scheduled and Dr. Howard gave my master and mistress the results around 1:00 p.m.

"Bad news, Mr. Hill. You have a large malignant tumor in your colon and it's got to come out."

"How do you know without testing?" Jerry asked.

"I can tell by shape, size, and location. Do you have a surgeon?"

Jerry answered immediately, "No. Will you help me find one in a hurry? I tend to be a worrywart."

Thirty minutes later, Dr. Howard's nurse found that Dr. Matt had a cancellation at 2:00 p.m. and his office was only ten minutes away.

And so the worrywart and the concerned wife went to see Dr. Matt. They were instantly impressed and comfortable with him.

"I can schedule you in about ten days when I'm back from vacation."

"When do you leave?" Jerry asked.

"After surgery, tomorrow."

"Could you put me on your schedule, tomorrow?"

"I have a full schedule," he said hesitantly.

Jerry continued his pressure. "Doctor, I'm a big-time worrywart. I'll make you a proposition. I'm all cleaned out from the colonoscopy and ready for surgery. So I'll come in when your surgery patients come in tomorrow morning and if you can perform the surgery at the end of your schedule, great. If not, I'll be waiting when you return from vacation." Jerry took a deep breath.

"Mr. Hill, you're really serious? Okay. But no promises."

When they came home that afternoon, their worry was overwhelming. I sensed something immediately in Barb's behavior. My master tried to hide it, but I read him like a book and I was scared. They made arrangements for our neighbors to walk me, and early the next morning they left.

Barb arrived home late, but I could see that she was relieved. She mixed a drink and I sat near her, listening to her phone calls to friends and relatives. She seemed really upbeat, so I felt better. But where was my master?

Later that evening their son Chris arrived from North Carolina. A few days later, Tim showed up, and a few more days after that Mark arrived. Barb would have one of her sons every day on hand to help her and visit their dad.

They took me to the hospital every day, and I wore my therapy jacket. This was one of the hospitals where I had been making visits for several years, so I was delighted yet surprised to find my master lying in a hospital bed. I whined quietly and then gazed up into his face. He smiled and I met his dangling hand with my cold nose.

"Hi Shy," he said, rubbing my head gently. "You'd better not reject me because the results of the oncology report are still a few days off."

I had no idea what he was babbling about, but I could never reject my master. The bed was lowered and I attempted to get up even closer to Jerry on the bed, but Chris laughed and said, "No Shiloh. Don't crowd Dad."

Every day the nurses would bring other nurses to meet the famous therapy Dog. That's me in case you forgot. While they were there, they would ask Jerry, "Can we get you anything, Mr. Hill?" All that my master wanted was a signal, even a small fart to indicate that his re-sectioned gut was again working properly. Eventually it did work properly, and after being discharged he recovered at a miraculous rate.

The big news was to arrive a few days later from Dr. Paul, who said, "Mr. Hill, your cancer was a grade two and no radiation or chemo is recommended."

It was all Greek to me. I don't need too much information. I just needed to see their faces to read the message. I was so happy that my master was no longer sick and would be himself again.

CHAPTER 68

The Shootout

> *A priest made the sign of the cross before each putt
> and had great success. His friend asked, "Father, would
> it help my putting if I did the same?" "No!" the priest answered.
> "Why not?" "Because you're a lousy putter."*
>
> —Augie

A few days before my master's surgery he played golf and qualified for the Winter Shootout.

You might be wondering what a shootout is. Let me explain. Having listened to Jerry, his three sons, and his adopted godson, John, talk about it, I'm an expert on the subject. Mark is a PGA Pro, John is a member of the PGA Champions Tour, Tim's handicap is one, and Chris's handicap is eight, and Jerry…I've never heard his handicap. For a few months prior to the shootout, golfers at the Ocean Club turn in their scores with the ten best net scores qualifying for the event. These ten golfers all tee off on the first tee. The highest score on the first hole is eliminated. If there is a tie for the worst score, those golfers chip off from a spot determined by Joe the Pro. The owner of the ball that ends up farthest from the hole is eliminated. The remaining nine golfers tee off on the second hole, and the same procedure continues until there are only two golfers left when they reach the ninth hole.

The Winter Shootout was scheduled for late January. My master had made a remarkable recovery from his cancer surgery, but he wasn't allowed to play golf just yet.

On shootout day, a Monday, I got to go to the pro shop with my master. Since he couldn't compete, we rode on a golf cart and watched the match. The weather was ominous and just before the golfers were about to head to the first tee, the heavens opened and a monsoon followed.

"Sorry men," Joe the Pro said, "We'll re-schedule for next Monday."

The next Monday was like the movie, *Groundhog Day.* Joe again said, "Next Monday."

The following Monday, exactly forty days after Jerry's surgery, Jerry was allowed to play. I had to wait at the condo. With ten players starting, it took about three hours to complete a nine-hole shootout.

Restlessly, I paced up and down the living room and flopped on the floor, only to get up and begin pacing again.

They played the shootout on the front nine and since our condo was near the tenth green, I could see nothing from the windows. I would just have to wait and hope.

Finally my master walked in the door with a huge smile. I listened in awe as he explained to Barb what happened.

He survived a chip-off on the sixth hole and then hit his tee shot over the seventh green. Both Ken and Gene had very short birdie putts. Ed was twenty-five feet away, but he was getting a one-half-shot handicap and Jerry wasn't. We both waited expectantly. Barb wanted Jerry to give her the final result, but that wasn't his style. Out of a bad lie behind the seventh green he hit a poor shot, leaving him a seventy-foot putt for par. Jerry made it and then watched Ed roll up to within four feet. Ken and Gene made their birdie putts. Ed left his par putt one inch short and was eliminated. Jerry had survived.

Barb said impatiently, "Jerry, I'm going to the grocery store. All I want is the executive summary."

So Jerry finally delivered the good news. "I beat good friend, Gene on the last hole," he exclaimed with a huge smile.

"What would you like for dinner?" she replied. By now you can tell that Barb really isn't into golf.

In all fairness, at dinner Barb congratulated him on his victory but told him that she was more impressed with his remarkable recovery from cancer.

I was impressed with how lucky he was to have the two-week delay that allowed him to play. He definitely had some angels working on his side. Maybe there is something to that Friday the Thirteenth magic, as the shootout took place on that date.

Like Barb, I was also very grateful and astonished at his quick recovery.

CHAPTER 69

Church Revisited

May there always be an Angel by your side.

—Unknown

Shortly after the devastating earthquake in Haiti, Minister Randy and his assistant went on a mission trip for a week to help the people there. I've heard several people including my master say that they suspect that animals, Dogs in particular, can sense a change of weather or when an earthquake is about to occur. I myself have sensed some unrest deep within the structure of the earth, even as far away as we were from Haiti. Being a Dog, I wasn't able to warn anyone of my sensations from the earth, and in fact I didn't exactly know what I was sensing.

Before Randy and his assistant left, they organized the Sunday church services during their absence, with laypersons doing the service. We were asked if we would participate. Jerry said, "Sure, what would we do?" Everything is an adventure for my master. I'm going to tell you the entire story.

We arrived at church early. Jerry miked-up so that everyone could hear him. We hid in a room at the back of the Church, where no one would see us. We could hear the parishioners talking and soon we heard music playing. Then, suddenly Jerry perked up as a message came through his earphone.

"Up, Shiloh," Jerry said. "You're going on stage." The entire congregation was seated and facing toward the chancel. Jerry and I entered the church from behind, allowing us to get to the front before being seen. As we walked down the center aisle Jerry began talking. He's always talking, but I really liked what he was saying this time. "Shiloh, look at all these people. There's a huge crowd today. Of course you're probably not surprised. Your name, which comes from the bible, means the coming of the peacemaker. These people are all here to see you."

It finally dawned on me that my master was speaking into this microphone about me but he was really speaking for the benefit of the congregation.

By this time we had reached the chancel. This was my second time on-stage. This time instead of Minister Randy, Jerry was doing the talking. In all of the stories I have listened to over the course of my life about Jerry's adventures and self-avowed skills, ministering to the masses had never been mentioned. Later, I figured out that the prayer he was about to read was part of a sermon that was written by Randy's assistant. I don't mean to say that he couldn't have delivered a prayer on his own if he'd had to. My master was rarely at a loss for words.

He prefaced this prayer by introducing me. Sensing that the prayer was forthcoming, I dropped down on all fours in my praying posture. As with my previous performance, the congregation was filled with good-natured laughter.

As you know, Jerry is very wordy. He had taken so long to begin the prayer that I felt restless and impatient. About halfway through the prayer I got up and began wandering up the aisle, nuzzling people who were praying. Many of them petted me. I felt a critical eye upon me. I turned back and looked at Jerry. Although he was praying, his eyes were just high enough to catch my gaze and vice-versa. I was in trouble. Therapy Dogs are taught to never break out of a stay position. My only hope was that I would be forgiven because we were in church. I've never heard Jerry speak so fast and he appeared somewhat agitated as he sped up the remainder of the prayer. With great emphasis, he said, "Amen. Now, children and Shiloh, we're off to Sunday School."

CHAPTER 70

1,200 Visits

A gentle word of compliment falls lightly
but it carries great weight.

—Shiloh

O n Good Friday in 2010, I made my 1,200th hospice visit. It was two years after *Therapy Dogs Inc.* had presented me with a special medal for my 1,000th visit. Along with my service badges for my one, five, and ten years of therapy work, I wear this medal with great pride on my therapy vest.

To celebrate my newest accomplishment, I was the special guest of the Hospice of Treasure Coast at Willoughby Country Club for a recognition luncheon. With fifty women for every man, I thought to myself, "These are my kind of odds." Dr. Benson, the Hospice CEO, opened the luncheon with some very complimentary comments regarding my record achievement.

A wonderful luncheon followed, but unfortunately there was no food for me. I heard the usual ohs and ahs and, "We must get this recipe." Then came another introduction. A lovely lady paid me more compliments and introduced my mouthpiece, Jerry. He went to the speaker's podium and I was ushered in my 'on heel' mode to a floor seat nearby, in a spot where everyone could observe me. I felt a bit of pressure being up front and on the stage. I laid my head between my forepaws and with my brown eyes I watched my master perform brilliantly.

He highlighted my career of over ten years of volunteer work at hospices, hospitals, rehab centers, Alzheimer's clinics, adult day care centers, senior centers, elementary schools, Homework Angels, church services, church visits, and museum visits. It was quite a long list of places I have done service over the years. Normally I'd fall asleep as he droned on, but it did remind me of all the good I'd done and I felt proud of myself.

Finally he finished talking and the majority of the crowd lined up to shake my paw, pet me, and shower me with a few more well-deserved compliments. I did hear a few women discussing how great the food was. It then dawned on me that I had received lots of compliments but no food. So goes a Dog's life.

Eileen Dito is the Volunteer Coordinator of the Treasure Coast Hospice and she has given new meaning to the word *volunteer*. With Eileen's permission, I am sharing this with you:

Valuable is the work you do
Outstanding is how you come through
Loyal, sincere and full of good cheer
Untiring in your efforts throughout the year
Notable are the contributions you make
Trustworthy in every project you take
Eager to reach every goal
Effective in the way you fulfill each task
Ready with a smile like a shining star
Special and wonderful, that is what you are.

CHAPTER 71

Doggone Good Couple a Days
A Single Rose

The world is full of beautiful things, this everyone knows,
but most of them pale in comparison to the beauty
of a single rose. This rose we give to you to let you
know we care about you. May it brighten your
day and bring you joy in everything you do.

—Rotary Club of Stuart

I was a special guest at the New York Mets exhibition
baseball game with the Washington Nationals. I was
both excited and curious. The Hospice of Treasure Coast
was being recognized for their good deeds and this hospet
Dog had a special assignment three hours before the cry of
'Play Ball' would start the game.

The Mets spring training instructors and I formed a
team to help the kid's clinic. While the KIDS waited their
turn to learn batting, fielding, and base running, I was the

warm-up act to keep them busy. I decided to show them my speed around the bases but was quickly escorted to the bench.

After going to the clinic, we entered the main stadium, where Jerry received supper and I received zero. The smell of hot Dogs and pizza was overwhelming but there were no rewards for the warm-up Dog.

From high up in our seats between home plate and third base, I watched the major leaguers play. "WOOF!" I shouted. These guys are good, I thought. After a few innings we headed out to our car. Jerry, who is always very sure of himself, couldn't find our vehicle. It was a hot evening and we were both Doggone tired. But, it's not in Jerry's DNA to ask for help.

I sniffed a few tires and left my mark, but we had no luck in finding our vehicle. Finally the lights flashed on and off a few rows away and we stumbled to our truck. Then we went home to eat and go to bed. I slept long and well.

The next day, I was on the road again. This time we went to the Stuart Rotary Club, where I was a special guest for the second day in a row. After another lunch that was only for the humans, my master and I were introduced and my incredible record was repeated once again. To my surprise I was given ten dozen roses in recognition of my exemplary volunteer achievements. We were asked to give them to the people whom we visit at our various venues.

First we delivered two dozen roses to a church office, where they would redistribute to parishioners. Next we visited an Alzheimer's group, where there was no confusion when we gave each of them a beautiful red rose. We then arrived at the Parkway Rehab Center, where Nina Brown from chapter sixty-five resides. We began giving the roses to the residents and then my master had a more productive idea. He decided to give a dozen roses to a few staff members, who were to each keep one and distribute the rest. Jerry is always thinking. He must have been a superb delegator in his working days.

Three hours later we had distributed all but one dozen of the gorgeous flowers. The full day of work had been a whirlwind and this Dog was tired but very happy. The next day we gave each Guatemalan girl at Homework Angels a rose and all of them gave me a hug. KIDS and Roses made for a doggone good couple a days.

CHAPTER 72

Carson's Fundraiser

*Each day is a gift and
each moment is precious.*

—Unknown

Every May before we leave Florida, we get involved in Carson's annual cancer fundraiser. Once Jerry became a Cancer Survivor, this event became even more meaningful.

I talked about Carson in chapter 34. His dad died of colon cancer and this year is the tenth year of the Memorial Golf Tournament raising money to help cancer patients. Ten years ago he started the event as a way of celebrating the memory of a beloved father, and it has since turned into one of the most successful and popular charity golf tournaments on the Florida Treasure Coast. The event has raised $416,000 to help cancer patients by providing them access to sophisticated treatments at the Cancer Center at Martin Memorial Health Systems.

Carson and his sister, Beth, run the tournament over a two-day period, including a dinner reception at Carson's Tavern on the Friday night before the Saturday tournament.

I get involved in three ways: I go with my master to the planning meetings, I have Jerry write a check so that my name is on a tee marker. It's kind of like the TV show *Cheers* because everyone knows my name, and I go to the big wingding reception the night before the event, which is my favorite part.

There are so many people there that a person can hardly move. But it's no problem for me as I curl under a table and out of the traffic flow, hoping for a few tidbits that fall my way on the floor. I've even had folks crawl under the table to get a closer look. Unfortunately, I don't get invited to the tournament itself.

My master feels very strongly about this event and the good that it does. We're both big believers that everyone should give back in this world. It's very interesting because the more you give, the more you get back, but you should not do it for that reason. Giving and receiving are the same.

Here's my challenge to all masters and their Dogs: get involved. Through this book you can get lots of ideas. There are a zillion additional ideas just waiting for your team to discover. Don't wait any longer. Get involved now.

CHAPTER 73

My Favorite Stops

*The reason a Dog has so many friends is
that he wags his tail instead of his tongue.*

—Unknown

We headed back to Michigan later than usual. Barb and Jerry were avoiding the Michigan cool springs more and more, so we almost went from Florida's spring right into a Michigan summer.

I will be turning thirteen this year, and Jerry has convinced me that it's a lucky number since he was born on Friday the Thirteenth. I sure hope he's right because I'm really slowing down and sleeping a lot. But I still enjoy my favorite stops.

Our first stop was the Glenn Post Office, where I always get a biscuit from Diane or Jackie, and then we went to The Glenn, my favorite breakfast restaurant. I sat under the table while my master read the mail and drank coffee from his bottomless coffee mug.

The regulars all knew me, and they even asked me questions. I would have loved to borrow a line from the movie *Hop* or *Zookeeper* and actually answer them out loud. But that wouldn't be believable. Or maybe it would.

"Wake up, Shy!" I heard my master say. The Gerstner Hardware store was our next stop. Founded in 1946, it is owned by Vickie and managed by my friend Rhonda, and I found it amazing that it was able to compete with the other more modern hardware stores. With only a blinker light to slow traffic motoring through Glenn, the hardware store depended on the locals and farmers of the area for business. The inventory included some truly unique items from the 1940s.

I wandered around the store under the watchful eye of the biggest yellow cat I've ever seen. "Do I look like a shoplifter?" I thought to myself. Maybe he thinks I'll eat his food in his bowl in the corner. I might if I thought I could get away with it.

Jerry's voice takes precedent when he says, "Shy, forget the cat. Get back in the truck. We're off to Saugatuck."

On the way to Saugatuck we pass the Glenn Salon. Lisa, a perky and petite redhead, is the owner. I think we weigh about the same, which is seventy-five pounds. I'd love to paw-wrestle her for a free summer trim. But we passed by the Glenn Store, which is operated by Coreen and Terese, who serve the best deli food from here to Chicago.

"Good news," I thought to myself as Jerry picked up a prescription at the Saugatuck Drugs. Mark, a University of Michigan fan, owned the store, and before we received our script, he talked about football with my master. Janet invited me to the old time soda fountain inside the drugs store, for a spoon sample of my favorite vanilla ice cream, and it was a great treat.

After that we went across the street to the bank. My master opened the door and I busted in with my short leash in my mouth and gave a muted howl, which evoked laughter from employees and customers alike. I pushed open the swinging door and waited behind each teller for my treat. As I approached the drive-in teller, she dropped something on the floor and bent over to find it. I put my paws up on the counter just as an elderly lady stopped her car across from me. I'll never forget the expression on her face. It was so frightening that I got down just as the teller straightened up. Jerry was watching directly in line with the drive-in window, and he reported that the lady's second shock came as she saw the previously missing teller. I love to hear my master tell this story whenever the bank hires a new teller.

I wished it was lunch-time, because we would have been choosing between my two favorite watering holes, Phil's Bar and Grille and Wally's, two of Saugatuck's best restaurants. But there was no time so we left.

Our last stop was the Dutch Market. Farmer Ed owns the place and he's the best. Unfortunately, his wife Ardith died prematurely a few years ago. She created the Shiloh cup of ice cream. Jerry sat in a rocking chair on the front porch while he drank his coffee. My Shiloh cup was between his feet and I enjoyed my special treat from the Dutch Market. Everyone missed Ardith, including the many young people she taught during her more than thirty years as a teacher.

My goal is to touch as many lives as I can during the remainder of my years and value all of my experiences.

CHAPTER 74

The Bigger House

Go Blue

—Fielding H. Yost

Jerry never had a chance. He was destined to become part of the legacy of maize and blue, which were the colors of the University of Michigan.

His dad left the Upper Peninsula of Michigan in 1916 to enroll in the Engineering School at the University of Michigan in Ann Arbor.

He was seventeen years old and it was his first time visiting the lower peninsula. He was a true Yooper, as people from the Upper Peninsula are called, and until the Mackinac Bridge was built in 1959, he never heard the term *trolls* used to describe people who live in the Lower Peninsula.

This seven-mile long bridge connected the two peninsulas for the first time in history and it came into vogue to describe those living below the bridge as trolls.

When Jerry's dad arrived in Ann Arbor, he was a bit homesick and overwhelmed by this great university, until he discovered that they had a hockey team. In those days it was a club sport, but every bit as competitive as the NCAA teams that followed. Having lived in Sault St. Marie, Michigan, across the river from Canada, he had played hockey for all of his life. He was one of the top players and he never got homesick again. Jerry likes to tell the story of how his dad made one round trip annually on the train to Ann Arbor. He was the oldest sibling in a large family and back then no one considered taking a trip home for the holidays. Times have changed since then.

My master had been an Eagle Scout, which allowed him to attend the University of Michigan football games. The scouts helped people find their seats and then the scouts sat on the concrete steps when the game began. He still tells anyone who will listen about his first game, which was Army vs. Michigan. They were ranked number one and number two, respectively, and Army beat Michigan with their great running backs: Mr. inside, Doc Blanchard and Mr. outside, Glen Davis. It was right after World War II and the Army team was loaded with great players. My master was hooked.

When he left his small high school to attend Michigan in 1952, Jerry was confident that he would make both the basketball and tennis teams. He was wrong, but he still fell in love with everything connected to the maize and blue.

The summer of 2010 seemed to drag for Jerry until the football frenzy of fall came. After forty years, he had given up his season tickets, so he instead parked himself on Saturdays in front of the TV, armed with his maize-and-blue sponge brick that was inscribed with the phrase: "Bad-Call Brick."

I began watching the games with him, and I was intrigued with the quarterback, Mr. Robinson, number sixteen. I have never seen anyone who can run and dodge the opponents like he can. Dogs can run like the wind, but humans usually can't. This man was truly electrifying and I wondered if I could have outrun him in my younger years. He ran and passed for more yardage than any quarterback in college history. Better yet, he seemed like a nice, humble young man when he was being interviewed.

During the last few years, Michigan Stadium, the largest stadium in the country, has gone through expansions, and a quarter of a billion dollars have been spent on its renovation. The capacity is 109,901, and the one seat is for Fielding H. Yost, the legendary coach of the 1910s and 1920s. He's probably looking down from a higher perch than the press box, saying "Go Robinson, Go Blue."

CHAPTER 75

The Golden Years

*The greatness of a nation and its moral progress
can be judged by the way its animals are treated.*

—Mahatma Gandhi

As I reach the last plateau of my life, I prefer to think about all the good things rather than what may lie ahead in senior Dog status.

I've been happy for all of my life, living with a wonderful and supportive family. I've been lucky to be born an American Dog in the greatest country in the world. Having been born in 1998 as a Golden Retriever, rather than centuries earlier as a wolf, I've had great timing.

I've always had nutritious food and clean water, rather than having to forage through the forest for my next meal or drink from polluted streams.

I've been called handsome and beautiful, and modestly, I must say, it's true. I've lived on beautiful Lake Michigan near Wau-Ke-Na, the forest by the water. I've been allowed to roam with my master, sensing and smelling the great outdoors.

A world-class trainer, Sherry, trained me, using only positive reinforcement methods. She emphasized this method by showing me what to do and rewarding me for getting it right. My master and I have continued with this philosophy, and we've always had cooperation and never have any confrontation.

I've been called the friendliest Dog people have ever known. I've been allowed to prewash the dishes before they go into the dishwasher.

I've been allowed to stay outside on my own and welcome everyone who approaches the house.

I've gathered sticks from the woods and made my own depository on the front deck.

I've been able to go down the sixty-one steps and go for a swim in Lake Michigan whenever I want to.

I've been allowed on the couches.

I've been allowed to be the fourth or fifth member on golf outings and ride in the cart.

I've been used as a wake-up call for Grandma Barb.

I've found hundreds of tennis balls washed up on the beach and I've kept them all.

I've carried everyone's shoes all over the hunting cabin and no one has complained.

I've been permitted to roll over and rub my back, whether I'm in the house or outside in the grass or weeds.

I've been allowed to lie on tennis courts and retrieve any balls that go over the fence.

I would say that I have had a fantastic life, and I have experienced life with the best master in the world. I have had a blessed purpose in my life and I don't regret one thing.

CHAPTER 76

Spirit of 76

It's not how old you are but how you are old.

—Marie Dressler

Y ou can't control the length of your life, but you can control its depth.

When we started working on this book, my master Jerry remarked, "Shiloh, you and I are the same age and we're not getting any younger, so let's get moving." As Satchel Paige once said, "Don't look back. Someone may be gaining on you."

The same age? Was this Jerry's own special math? "Shiloh," my master says, "normal Dog to human years are a 7 to 1 ratio, but you're exceptional and therefore you receive a 10 percent bonus in years that brings your 7 years to 6.3."

I was twelve when we started this book, so 12 x 6.3 = 76, so Shiloh is seventy-six years of age, and 76 x 1.0 = 76, so Jerry is also seventy-six years of age.

Darn if he isn't right again. We're the same age.

Mark Twain once said, "Life could be infinitely happier if we could be born at age eighty and gradually approach eighteen."

My master and I are happy, even though we're much closer to eighty than to eighteen.

Many humans and Dogs of our age sit in a corner and vegetate, but not my master and me. Although we had never written anything before, we rejected staying in the sedentary corner. Instead we chose to tell my story. I hope you enjoyed reading it. Perhaps you'll be inspired by a couple of young and old codgers and undertake a project on your personal bucket list.

As Erma Bombeck said, "When we stand before God at the end of our lives, we would hope that we would not have a single bit of talent left and can say we used everything that God gave us."

Shiloh and Jerry

LATER

People often ask Jerry, "Why do you spend so much time with Shiloh?" My master responds, "I want no regrets when he's gone."

Another frequently asked question is "What's Shiloh going to do when he retires from therapy work?"

With a twinkle in his eye, Jerry answers, "I'll get him a greeter's job at Walmart."

MANY THANKS

Without the assistance of the people mentioned here, my book couldn't have happened. They all gave invaluable suggestions and expertise to help mold this memoir into a chronicle of my memories and experiences.

First, thank you to our editors, Dr. Frank Paparello and Barb Welk, for their editorial assistance with the manuscript.

Thanks to Pearl Kastran Ahnen, an established author, who gave us ideas and support.

Others supporting the preparation of this memoir include Franca Giuliani, the Quotation Queen, and Amy Lombardi, who gave us much encouragement and stated that my experiences would make a great book! Kathleen Oldford gave us unique insight into Dog and human relationships. Joe Ryan provided a special place in his Golf Pro Shop in Florida for my master to work on the book. Jennie Dailey is a Dog lover who inspired us, and Gene Popp never stopped reassuring us to continue, while Kendall and Craig, Jerry's copying experts, gave great service and encouragement.

A special thanks to Eileen Dito, Volunteer Coordinator of the Treasure Coast Hospice in Stuart, Florida, and all of her staff who inspired us to write. Many thanks to Minister Randy Hase and Assistant Minister, Barbara McMannis of Stuart Congregational Church for their great support and friendship.

In a wonderful gourmet restaurant called Salt of the Earth this book began its creation as my master Jerry and his co-author Colleen sat drinking coffee and working on the pages of the manuscript. Thanks to owners, Mark Schrock and Steve Darpel, for allowing us to spend long hours there.

To Jillian Mead and David Blauw of Holland Hospital, a big thank you for your support and enthusiasm. And thanks to Gail Curcio, an artist who captured my handsome likeness.

My veterinarians, who have kept me in good health over the years, deserve a word of thanks: Jim Barron, Pete VanVranken, James Havenga, Richard Smith, and Reed Claunch. A special debt of gratitude to Sherry who recognized my potential and trained me to be a successful Therapy Dog. Thanks to my master's son, Chris Hill, for his contributions.

And last but not least, thanks Mistress Barb for accepting the Dog that was not supposed to be part of the family. I am very sorry for the pain I have caused you because of your fall. And thank you for never blaming me.

Thanks to the many others who encouraged and supported this book, including the former English teacher, Karen Hickman, who wanted to help.

Shiloh

ABOUT THE AUTHORS

SHILOH is a medium-colored golden retriever who was born on June 4, 1998. He has been doing extensive volunteer therapy work for over twelve years. This is his first book.

JERRY HILL retired from Bill Knapp's restaurants in 1992 as its president and CEO. He now does volunteer work and plays lots of golf. He splits his time between Lake Michigan and Stuart, Florida, with his wife, Barb. This is his one and only book.

COLLEEN RAE has published two novels, *Mohave Mambo* and *Chihuahua Enchilada*. She is presently working as a correspondent for a newspaper in Saugatuck, Michigan, and she lives near Lake Michigan. When she isn't writing, she spends her spare time with her husband and life partner, Larry, and her three cats, Bubba Bear, Samantha, and Kali.

To order additional copies: www.shilohspeaksthebook. com or www.colleenraesnovels.com